FOREVER FAMILY

River's End Ranch Book 26

KIRSTEN OSBOURNE

Copyright © 2017 by Kirsten Osbourne

All rights reserved.

No part of this book may be reproduced in any form or by any electronic or mechanical means, including information storage and retrieval systems, without written permission from the author, except for the use of brief quotations in a book review.

INTRODUCTION

After thirty-five years of peaceful marriage, Bobbi and Wilber Weston have come to a crossroads. They each want something different, and neither is willing to give in to the other. Bobbi loves her children and grandbabies more than she'd ever imagined, and she doesn't think asking for a change in the plans she'd made with Wilber many years ago should be a difficult thing.

Wilber has been waiting his entire life to get the monkey off his back so he can travel, but now his wife has other plans for their future. He doesn't understand why they can't continue with their goals as they were doing before the children married and procreated. Will the two of them be able to make a compromise that will please them both? Or will their marriage end up being just another ugly statistic?

1

Bobbi Weston glared at her husband of almost thirty-five years. "I know we agreed to keep traveling the country in our RV, but do you realize I have three grandbabies here with more on the way? How can I leave my precious babies?"

Wilber shook his head. "We've done our time with children and on the ranch. I love it here as much as you do, but I don't want the kids to think they can come running to us every time there's a little problem with the ranch. We raised six kids. We can be grandparents a couple of weekends a year."

She sighed. "I thought I could live with that plan, but I really can't. I *need* to be with them. I want them to know me." How could he not understand how much those grandbabies meant to her?

"After thirty-four years of raising children, don't you think we deserve a break?"

"Of course we do, but we've taken one. We've been gone for over a year. Now that we're back, I want to stay. I want to be with my grandchildren. The twins are so precious, and they're getting excited when they see me now. How can you possibly want to leave?"

"How can you *not?* This is what we've been working for our entire lives!"

Bobbi sighed. "I know that's what we said, but that was before the *grandbabies*."

Wilber shook his head, walking toward the door of the cabin. "I've got a quick meeting with Pastor Kevin. We'll stay through the vow renewal at the end of the month, but then I'm done. I need my freedom."

After the door closed behind her husband, Bobbi sank into a chair, wondering why she'd married the man in the first place. He was bossy, annoying, and absolutely impossible.

Even as the thought crossed her mind, she thought of her first moments on the ranch. This place was in her blood as much as it was in his.

She'd been only eighteen and already on her own. After her father had shot her mother in a fit of jealous rage when she was eight, she'd bounced from foster home to foster home. Immediately after her high school graduation, she'd packed the few clothes she had into her backpack and started walking with no destination in mind. She'd worked a couple of short-term jobs, taken a few buses from place to place, and she'd been ready for adventure.

The first thing she'd done after getting to the ranch was go to lunch at Kelsey's Kafé, grinning at the alliteration caused by the creative spelling. She sat down for lunch and counted the money she had left, which was less than five dollars. Frowning down at the menu, she chose a bowl of soup and a glass of water. Hopefully she'd have a job before she needed to eat again. She could sleep in the woods, since it was summertime, but food was necessary for life.

A woman in her late forties stopped at her table. "What can I get for you today?"

"Soup of the day and a glass of water, please."

The woman frowned at her. "You're too skinny as it is. You need to eat a real meal." She called back toward the kitchen. "Get me today's special and a bowl of soup!"

Bobbi's jaw dropped. "I can't afford that." What kind of waitress wouldn't let her have what she wanted to eat, anyway?

"It's on the house. If you're that worried about it, you can wash some dishes this afternoon."

"I'll wash dishes, then." Bobbi wasn't about to take handouts from anyone. Her last foster mother had made it clear that she was a burden, and they'd only taken her in because of the money the state paid them for her. She wasn't going to be a burden on anyone else for as long as she lived.

"Suit yourself." The older woman walked away, coming back a minute later with a big bowl of soup and a basket of crackers. "Get started on that." She stood and watched as Bobbi ate her first bite, nodding with satisfaction.

Bobbi decided to ignore her. She obviously thought she was in charge of the place...but if she was, she wouldn't be waiting tables, would she? She pulled a book out of her backpack and opened to the page she'd bookmarked—with a real bookmark. She'd had a friend who had thought dog-earing the pages was just as good as a bookmark, but she'd been very wrong.

The woman stood and watched her eat and read for a minute, and then she'd slid into the booth across from her. "I'm Kelsey Weston."

"As in Kelsey from Kelsey's Kafé?" Maybe the woman was acting as if she owned the place because she did.

"The very one. Where are you headed?"

Bobbi shrugged. "I really don't know." She didn't offer more information, because she'd found that no matter how curious people were, they didn't want to hear her story about leaving the foster home. And no one wanted to hear that her father had shot her mother. Who would?

"Would you consider staying on here for a little while? I can give you a small room in the ranch house, and you can help out here."

Bobbi swallowed another bite of the tomato soup. It was delicious. "What would you want me to do?"

"Dishes. Bus tables." Kelsey watched her carefully, obviously sizing her up.

Bobbi nodded. "I can do that."

"I'll show you to your room after you wash dishes this afternoon, then. Minimum wage, but you get one meal a day here in the diner, and you have a room to stay in as long as you're working here."

"Sounds fair." Bobbi had no idea why the woman wanted her to work there, but she needed the job. Badly.

Another woman stopped at the table. "You hire her yet?" the woman asked. She seemed about the same age as Kelsey Weston.

"Yes, Jaclyn, I hired her. She's going to wash dishes and bus tables. Are you happy now?"

Jaclyn shrugged. "The fairies say she's the one." The woman turned and walked away, leaving Bobbi staring after her.

"Who was that?" Bobbi asked.

Kelsey sighed. "That's my best friend, Jaclyn Hardy. She's in charge of the RV park."

"She seems a bit...odd." Bobbi smiled as she realized the second part of what Kelsey Weston had said. "You have an RV park here on the ranch? I've always wanted to have an RV so I could travel around the country."

Kelsey smiled. "My son, Wilber, says the same thing. He's not at all pleased that he's in charge of this ranch until his children are old enough to take over."

"How old are his children?" Bobbi asked, wondering about the people who she'd be working for.

"Oh, he isn't even married yet. That might be the problem." Kelsey stood up and brushed off her apron. "I didn't catch your name."

Bobbi knew she hadn't thrown it, but since the woman would be her employer, she probably should. "I'm Bobbi Jackson."

"Welcome to River's End Ranch, Bobbi. Not everyone who comes here finds what they're looking for, but I have a feeling you will." Kelsey turned and walked away, leaving Bobbi staring after her.

What an odd person. Bobbi turned her attention back to her book and her soup. At least the food was good.

Bobbi shook her head, walking to the window of the cabin. There was no use in dwelling on the past. She loved the ranch and everything about it, just as much as she'd loved it when she first arrived all those years ago. Kelsey Weston had been the best mother-in-law a woman could ask for, but Jaclyn had been her real mentor. Maybe it was time to pay the old woman a visit.

WHEN BOBBI UNLATCHED JACLYN'S GATE AND STEPPED INTO her yard, she wasn't at all surprised that Jaclyn stepped out onto her front porch. "The fairies told me you were coming. Do you realize you were my first match? There was something about you that made the fairies start talking to me."

Bobbi felt her lips curve up. She'd seen Jaclyn several times since she and Wilber had come back to the ranch, but she hadn't visited her. "How many bunnies do you have this week?"

"Twenty-four. Got them all fixed, though, so hopefully

there won't be a lot more of them." Jaclyn held her door wide open. "Come in. I made tea and snickerdoodles. You still like snickerdoodles, don't you?"

Bobbi smiled, feeling a sense of déjà vu. She'd been here so many times over the years to visit her mother-in-law's closest friend. After Kelsey's death, she'd kept Bobbi going. "Of course, I still like snickerdoodles. Who doesn't?"

Jaclyn cackled softly. "Get in this house!"

Bobbi stepped inside, pushing a bunny out of her way as she sat down. "I see you've matched up all of my children, and you've got years to go before you start on my grandbabies."

"There are guests and ranch employees. Now that I have the fairies on my side, no match is too difficult." Jaclyn poured tea for the two of them, and Bobbi took a cup. "Now, tell me what's really on your mind. You're not really thinking of leaving Wilber, are you?"

If anyone else had asked her that, Bobbi would have been shocked, but Jaclyn had always seemed to have the ability to read her mind. She claimed it was the fairies, of course, but Bobbi wasn't so sure. "Leaving him? I don't know. We've been married for almost twice as long as I was alone. What would I do without him?"

"Live here with your grandbabies." Jaclyn put her teacup down with a clatter. "Bobbi, Wilber is the man who you're destined to be with. If you don't stay married to him, you're going to be unhappy. The fairies say you need to work things out."

Bobbi frowned. "That's just the thing. I don't know if we can work this one out. He never understood that I was attracted to his family as much as I was to him. Having a big family—and being loved—it was so important to me. It still is. He wants me to leave my grandbabies, and I just don't think I can do that."

Jaclyn studied her for a moment. "Surely two grown adults who have been together for almost thirty-five years can make compromises. Don't you think?"

"You want me to compromise on my grandchildren? Do you know what you're asking?"

"Your children have been like grandchildren to me. I can't imagine any of them going anywhere. Since Kelsey died, I've been lonelier, and your children have kept me going. When you left, it was like losing my own daughter, so yes, I do know what I'm asking." Jaclyn leaned forward and took Bobbi's hand in a firm grip. "I also know you and Wilber are meant to be together. Nothing should keep you apart."

Bobbi frowned. She knew that Jaclyn had lost her only love many years before. "And you're sure the fairies are never wrong?" Bobbi didn't believe in the fairies...exactly. She did believe in Jaclyn, though.

"They didn't start talking to me until right before you arrived on the ranch, you know. You were the catalyst. You have to know how much it means to me that the two of you work things out. I guess you could come here and talk to me with him...like a marriage counselor!"

Bobbi blanched at the very idea. "I think we'll be fine without going to those extremes."

"I'm willing if you need me."

"I really appreciate it." Bobbi got to her feet before she found herself consenting to something no sane human being would *ever* agree to. "I'm going to head over to Kelsi's. I want to play with my grandbabies. Willow and Tori need grandma kisses to grow, you know."

Jaclyn waved her away. "Just remember the offer stands!"

Bobbi said a silent prayer she would never be that desperate. She'd rather stick a fork in her own eye than go to Jaclyn for counseling. Maybe Pastor Kevin could help, though... With a wave, she headed out the door. As she walked, she thought back again to her first day on the ranch. She spent the afternoon washing dishes as she'd promised, but after the café closed, she walked with Mrs. Weston over to the main ranch house. "My family lives here, but we have a room you can use," the older woman explained.

"You want me to live with your family?" Bobbi had asked, her eyes wide. "Are you sure?"

"Are you a drug addict or a mass murderer? Will you rob us blind?"

"Well, no...but my father murdered someone."

Mrs. Weston stopped walking for a moment, looking Bobbi up and down. "I don't believe the sins of the fathers should be taken out on the child. Do you?"

"Well, no. But they have been."

"How so?"

Bobbi sighed, wondering just how much she should reveal to this woman. Her entire life people had looked at her oddly because they knew the truth about her. Finally, she decided she shouldn't hide it. This woman was being kind enough to offer her a job and a place to stay. She owed it to her. "My father killed my mother in a drunken fit when I was eight. He went to jail, and I've spent my life in foster homes. I left the day I graduated."

"How long ago was that?"

"Only about a month."

Mrs. Weston frowned. "You've been on your own for a month? Where have you lived?"

Bobbi shrugged. "Here and there. I have worked for long enough to travel. I want to see all the states. I'd never left Oklahoma before, and now I've been to Texas, New Mexico, Arizona, Utah, and Idaho." She looked around her at the mountains and the beautiful land. "I think Idaho is the most beautiful of them all."

"It's also the coldest. You need to be settled before winter, my young nomadic friend." Mrs. Weston wrapped her arm around Bobbi's shoulders and began walking toward the house again.

"You don't want me to leave?"

Mrs. Weston laughed. "Of course, I don't. My friend, Jaclyn, says that you're meant to be here."

"The crazy woman who said something about fairies at lunchtime?"

"That very one. She's been a true friend to me. She would have married my brother, but he died in the line of duty. He was a police officer."

Bobbi frowned. "I'm so sorry."

"It's been a very long time, my dear." Mrs. Weston shook her head. "I declare that the rest of the evening is for talking about happy things. Nothing negative."

"That sounds good to me."

"While you settle into your room, I will make a feast. My husband and son work many hours and they're famished when they finally arrive home at the end of a long day."

"What do they do?" Bobbi asked. Although she'd grown up in Oklahoma, she knew nothing about ranching. She'd spent her entire life in a small city.

Kelsey Weston smiled. "Why, they run the ranch, of course. I have three other sons as well, but they're married and no longer live on the ranch. I thought my children would run the place together someday, but it doesn't seem to be happening."

"And what do you do?"

"The café is mine. I've always wanted to have my own place, and I opened it after the children were grown. That's why I can just hire you without talking to anyone. It's completely my domain, even though it's on the ranch." Mrs. Weston stopped in front of a large ranch house. "I raised my children here. Don't you think this is a beautiful place to raise children?"

Bobbi nodded uncertainly. She had no idea what a good place to raise children would be. "I believe it would be."

Mrs. Weston led Bobbi to a room around the corner and opened the door. "This is our guest room. I hope you'll enjoy staying here." Then she was gone.

Bobbi bit her lip, looking around the pink-flowered room. It wasn't exactly what she'd have chosen for herself, but it wasn't awful. And it was a free room. She couldn't forget that. She'd slept outside too many nights since leaving Oklahoma. Tonight, she'd sleep in a soft bed under a roof. She couldn't let herself complain about that.

———

AFTER NAPPING FOR AN HOUR, BOBBI FELT A LOT BETTER. She was still exhausted from the long bus ride up from Salt Lake City, but she was determined not to let it show. She was starting a new life here at the ranch, and she was going to be happy.

A knock at her door startled her, but she hurried over and opened it wide. On the other side stood a man in his mid-twenties. He had dark hair and the most piercing ice blue eyes she'd ever seen. She felt like she could drown in them. "May I help you?"

The man seemed just as startled to see her as she was to see him. She didn't know how that was possible though, because he'd obviously been sent to fetch her. Surely someone had told him who she was. "Hi. I'm Wilber. My mother told me to bring you to dinner."

"Wilber? Like the pig in *Charlotte's Web*?" She did her best not to giggle. It wasn't polite to laugh at someone else's name.

Wilber sighed. "Pathetic, isn't it? It's been the tradition in my family to give all boys W names for generations."

"Really? Not the girls?"

He shook his head, offering her his arm. "May I escort you into the dining room for dinner, milady?"

She giggled. "Maybe you should just call me Bobbi. I'm the hired help around here. Nothing more."

"I don't know about that. You're the first person who's worked for the ranch Mom has invited to live here."

"Really? She acted like it was something she did every day."

Wilber frowned. "Not at all. She said something about Jaclyn liking you and needing you to stay."

"I met her. She's...odd."

He laughed. "She is. She's been Mom's best friend since before she married Dad, though. She's pretty awesome."

"If you say so..."

They got to the table and Mrs. Weston motioned for Bobbi to sit down. "We're not formal around here. It's hard to have manners when you spend your days taking care of animals and guests."

Bobbi realized she was sitting beside Wilber, and she smiled at him. "I like your ranch. Well, what I've seen of it."

"Tomorrow's Sunday and the diner is closed. Wilber, after church, you need to take her on a hike. The mountains are so beautiful this time of year. She needs to see our home in all its glory." Mrs. Weston sat in a chair and handed a bowl of mashed potatoes to Bobbi.

Bobbi noticed an older man at the other end of the table then. He must be Mr. Weston. "Oh, Wilber shouldn't have to spend his day off showing me around. I can hike up there myself."

Mrs. Weston shook her head. "No, there are bears and moose running around here. You need to be safe."

"No Bigfoot? Someone promised me I'd find Bigfoot in Idaho," Bobbi said, her eyes twinkling.

Wilber grinned. "I'm willing to look for him if you are."

"Sounds good to me. I wonder if he's friends with Jaclyn's fairies." She wanted to giggle at the idea, but she was afraid the others would be offended. "Does Jaclyn have any gnomes? I wonder if they'd ward off the fairies."

"I think we'll need to get her one. And I'm going to love spending my day off with you. I have a feeling you're going to make me laugh."

Bobbi looked at him and smiled. Humor had been what she'd fallen back on every day since her mother had died. If she could make people laugh, at least they wouldn't assume she was a killer too. It wasn't easy when the whole town knew your father killed your mother in a jealous rage.

Bobbi sighed, picking up the pace as she walked back to the cabin she was sharing with her husband to get her car. She would drive into Riston and see Kelsi and the twins. She'd had six children, and only the two youngest, twins, had been girls. She'd wanted a houseful of girls. Didn't the man determine the sex of the baby? Something else to be mad at Wilber for. She was keeping count. Who would have thought that after thirty-five years together she'd be so frustrated with him?

He'd seemed like such a charmer at first. And when the children had started coming, she'd thought her world would always be a perfect, idyllic place. How could she have been so wrong?

Unlocking the car door, she drove toward Riston, happy to be able to think about her grandbabies...and anything but her husband.

2

Sitting in Kelsi's living room with her and the grandbabies, Bobbi felt as if she was finally in her element. She snuggled baby Willow close, kissing her cheek softly. "Have I told you yet how glad I am you didn't name this sweet baby Widget?"

Kelsi grinned. "It was just a thought." She looked down at Tori sleeping in her arms. "I'm always surprised when she finally sleeps, because she wiggles so much, it seems that she never will."

"I understand. You were the same. Do you ever wish you'd had identical twins like you and Dani?"

Kelsi shook her head. "No way. I'm not sure how you put up with us. We hated looking alike so much, we'd do anything to look different. And I mean anything! There were days when Dani would smudge dirt on her face, just so we wouldn't look identical." She kissed the sleeping baby in her arms. "I wouldn't wish that on my two girlies for anything."

"I still have a hard time believing my youngest child was not only the first to give me grandbabies, but she doubled up the first time." As she said it, Bobbi wondered how her mother would have reacted to her own grandchildren, feeling sad that she'd never find out. For some reason, she'd started thinking about her mother more in the past few months.

"I was always ahead of my time! Besides, Ellie and Will are expecting, and so are Belinda and Wyatt. Pretty soon you're going to be drowning in grandbabies."

Bobbi smiled. "Nothing would make me happier, you know." She looked toward the window with a frown.

"Mom, what's wrong? I've never seen you look quite so...morose."

"Just trying to make some big decisions. Nothing for you to trouble yourself with."

Kelsi frowned at that. "I'm a pretty good listener."

"I know you are! You were the only one who listened to my Bigfoot theories and made them your own." Bobbi refused to let her time with her children and grandchildren be touched by sadness. No, she was going to make the most of every day.

A short while later, she headed back to the ranch. How was she going to be able to leave Riston and River's End Ranch again? The first time had been a necessity. They'd needed to make sure the kids were up for what they were taking on. An operation as big as the ranch was too much for most people. Their kids had made them proud, though.

She parked at the cabin before taking off into the woods. She needed to walk and think. Again, her mind went back the thirty-five years to 1982 when she was a new employee of the ranch, not a family member.

Bobbi had gone to church her first Sunday on the ranch, and she'd truly enjoyed it. The pastor in Riston had preached as if he knew people were real and not puppets, determined to do what they felt was right. He seemed to understand the struggles of being a teenager in the twentieth century. It was so different than her church in Oklahoma, where everyone was expected to be perfect in every way.

After the service, Wilber had taken her hand and helped her up into his big pick-up truck. There was a picnic basket in the middle of the big front seat. "I brought lunch. Do you ride?"

Bobbi shook her head. "I never had the opportunity to learn, though it's something I've always wanted to do."

"We'll take the ATVs then."

"What's an ATV?"

Wilber turned his head to look at her as he stopped at a stop sign. "Where are you from? Mars?" He shook his head. "An ATV has three wheels, and it's a small motorized vehicle. It stands for all-terrain vehicle. We can take a couple of ATVs up into the mountains. The view is unimaginable."

"Are they hard to drive?" she asked.

"Well, you drive a car, don't you?"

She shook her head. "My foster parents didn't think it was a skill that I needed."

"Of course, it is! I'll teach you myself." He frowned. "That makes it hard to take two ATVs up into the mountains, though. You'll have to share mine."

"Couldn't we just go for a walk?" She'd never been anywhere alone with a man. The foster parents she'd lived with since she was ten were religious nuts. They didn't think young people should date at all. She was surprised they hadn't made her wear a nun's habit. Over the time she'd been gone, she'd slowly started buying new clothes for herself, and she now dressed like most teens, though her clothes had been purchased in second-hand stores. At least she no longer felt conspicuous.

He frowned. "I guess we can. We won't be able to go as far up into the mountains, though. The view won't be quite as special."

She sighed. "I do like nice views." Thinking for a moment, she realized she no longer had to obey the strict rules she'd lived by for the past eight years. "I can share an ATV with you."

He grinned, reaching over to take her hand in his. "You're pretty special, aren't you?"

She blinked a few times at that. No one had ever thought she was special. "I'm not so sure about that..."

"I am. You're very special. When you smile, it feels like my whole world has lit up."

"Stop!" The car in front of them on the country highway slowed down a little and pushed a puppy out of the car.

He slammed on his brakes. "Did they just throw a dog out?"

She nodded, opening her door and running toward the animal. "Are you hurt? You poor thing!" She picked up the dog, who couldn't be more than a few months old, and cradled him in her arms. "How can people be so heartless?"

He shook his head. "I'll keep him until we can find him a new owner."

"I want him." She'd never had a pet. She'd never had anyone who would be hers forever, but this dog...he could be her forever family.

Wilber frowned. "I'm not sure Mom will let you keep him at the house."

"Where then? I need to keep him. I know this dog is meant to be mine!" She was almost frantic. She had to have him. "I guess I can move on if your mom won't let me take him into her house."

He frowned at her. "That dog is more important to you than having a job and a place to live? Really?"

There were tears streaming down her face, and she didn't bother to wipe them away. "Really. I need him."

He sighed. "All right. We'll go ask Mom if you can keep

him there. If not, I'll keep him at my cabin until you find somewhere else to live."

"You will?"

"Yup. I can see it's important to you, so I'll keep him."

"Don't you live with your parents?" No one had told her he did, but when he'd been there for dinner the night before, she'd just assumed.

"No. I live in a little cabin on the lake. It was built for guests, but Mom and Dad said I could stay there."

"So why were you at dinner last night?"

He shrugged. "Mom called me and invited me. She said she had a young guest staying there, and she thought you'd be more at ease if I was there too."

"She was right." She stood up from her crouched position, holding the puppy in her arms.

"Let's go ask Mom. I think our trip into the mountains today is shot regardless."

"Why?"

"Are you really willing to leave the puppy to go up there with me?"

She bit her lip. "Well..."

"I didn't think so. We'll go another time. Diner closes early. I'll take tomorrow afternoon off and pick you up at four."

"What about the puppy?"

He sighed. "We'll get him a collar and a leash and he can come along." He got back into the truck and started it, making a U-turn in the middle of the road. "Let's go talk to Mom."

When they got to the house, Bobbi carried the dog in her arms. They found Kelsey and Jaclyn sitting together in the living room, chattering away. They were obviously very close.

Kelsey looked up and saw Bobbi with the dog in her arms. "Where'd you get him?"

"We were going to go on an ATV up into the mountains, but the car in front of us slowed down and pushed him out. I couldn't let him get hit by a car!"

Kelsey sighed. "I guess you want to keep him here."

"I told her I'd keep him at the cabin if you won't let her." Wilber put his hand on Bobbi's shoulder, and she felt a tingle spread through her body. He really made her feel special.

"You can keep him." Kelsey shook her head, her gaze meeting Jaclyn's. "Do you see the sacrifices I make for you and your fairies?"

Bobbi wanted to squeal and jump up and down. "Thank you so much. I'll take good care of him."

"I know you will." Kelsey looked at her son. "Find Bandit's old bowls, would you? I'm sure we kept them somewhere. He's going to need a leash and a collar too."

"We'll go into town and find him something." He looked at Bobbi. "Do you want me to go alone? Or should we take him?"

"Is there a pet store in Riston? Or a place where we can get him what he needs?"

He shook his head. "We'd have to go further than Riston. Are you up for a Sunday drive?"

"With the dog?"

He nodded. "Sure, we can take him."

Bobbi smiled at Kelsey. "Thanks for letting me keep him. I promise I'll take good care of him." She hurried back out to the truck, ready to get her new baby what he needed. It was only after she was sitting in the truck that she remembered her financial situation. "I can't buy him anything. I have less than five dollars to my name." She was embarrassed to admit her financial situation, but he'd know soon enough.

"I'll get him what he needs."

"I'll pay you back when I get my first paycheck."

"Don't worry about it."

She glared at him, feeling a bit stubborn. "I won't let you pay for my dog."

He sighed. "I plan to be married to you before the end of the summer. What difference does it make if I start paying for the dog now or later?"

"You can't just announce you're going to marry me. It doesn't work like that!"

"Wanna bet?" He pulled the truck over to the side of the road and turned toward her, cupping her face in his hands. "I want to kiss you."

The dog chose that moment to stick his head between theirs, making her giggle. "I think Don Juan here wants my kisses more than you do."

He groaned. "I have a feeling I could prove you wrong about that."

She giggled some more. "I think he likes me."

"Of course he does. You've been holding him against you for a long time now. Hold me like that, and I'll like you too."

"Does that mean you don't like me now?" She batted her eyes playfully at him.

"Later, I'm going to take you for a walk, and show you just how much I do like you."

"Oh yeah?"

Wilber nodded. "I'm going to marry you, Bobbi. You might as well just agree now."

"You can't just announce you're going to marry me. You have to woo me. You have to propose on one knee on top of a mountain."

"On top of a mountain? I can make that happen pretty easily, you know."

"I do know." Bobbi scratched the dog's ears, realizing she liked the name Don Juan for him. She liked it a lot. "I can't make it too hard for you if I ever want to hear that proposal." For a moment, she daydreamed about what being married to him would be like. She'd get to keep him *and* his mother. They'd be her forever family, not just Don Juan. She liked the idea more than she cared to admit.

He grinned, pulling the truck back out onto the road. "I'll keep that in mind."

"You do that." She couldn't believe they were talking about marriage proposals when they'd never even kissed, but somehow it felt right. She belonged with this man, and she knew it with everything inside her.

Bobbi kicked at a rock at the edge of the lake, sending it back into the depths. She missed Don Juan, but more than that, she missed the man who had courted her with pretty words and promises of tomorrow. Where had he gone? Six kids later, he seemed so involved with everything and everyone around them. She couldn't even remember their last real date night. She missed their time together. All the while the kids had been growing up, they'd kept a weekly date night. It hadn't always happened on a Friday or Saturday night, but she understood that business owners couldn't always have the days they wanted off.

Now she'd give anything if he would just agree to let her spend more time with the grandbabies. She didn't know when he'd started seeing his own needs as more important than hers, but it had definitely happened. Maybe it had been gradual. Sometimes it was hard to tell.

As she walked back toward the cabin, she thought about Don Juan. She'd loved that dog with everything inside her. He'd been the first creature she'd given unconditional love to, and she'd received it back one hundred times over. He'd died when the twins were small, but all her boys had memories of playing with Don Juan.

Getting back into the cabin, she found Wilber sleeping on the couch, a book on his chest, snoring uproariously. Thirty-five years ago, she'd love to watch him sleep. He'd meant everything to her. Now every little thing he did annoyed her. The look on his face while he slept. The sound of his snores. Even the way he stretched first thing in the morning.

She sighed. She still loved him, and she knew she always would. The problem was she didn't like him much at the moment. Did that make her a bad person? She knew Kelsey would have thought so, but Kelsey had told her more than once that he was perfect when she had him. She had no idea what Bobbi had done to ruin him. The words had always made her want to strangle her mother-in-law, even though she'd loved her in a way that she wished she'd been able to love her own mother. Life was confusing.

Later that night while they were eating supper, he asked, "Do you have the plans in place for our vow renewal?"

Bobbi thought carefully about the words she wanted to say. She knew they would seem harsh, and that wasn't what she wanted at all. She just needed him to understand how she felt. "I'm not sure I want the vow renewal. I don't feel like we're in a good place right now."

He set down his fork. "What is that supposed to mean?"

"It means that we've changed. It means that you used to worry about my feelings first, and you'd do anything I needed to make me happy. It means that I'm tired and I'm crabby, and I don't know if I want to even be married to you anymore, let alone celebrate thirty-five years together as if everything is all hunky dory!"

"Are you telling me you want a divorce?" His face was full of emotions, shock being at the forefront.

"No. Not yet anyway. I think we need to try to work through what we're feeling though. I need to know why my feelings don't matter to you anymore. Maybe we should go to marriage counseling."

He shook his head. "No. We'll work it out together like

we always have." He balled up his napkin and threw it on the table. "I'm going for a walk."

As he left the cabin, she felt a tear slide down her face. She stood and cleared the table, doing the dishes. Even if she was in the depths of despair, she couldn't leave a mess in the kitchen. Once a dishwasher, always a dishwasher.

She went through the motions, hand-washing all the pots and pans and putting the dishes into the dishwasher. While she worked, she thought of her first real date with him, which came the Monday after they met.

Bobbi looked in the mirror in the bathroom at the back of the diner, making sure her hair wasn't coming out of her ponytail. It was, so she quickly brushed it into submission. The heat from the hot dishwater made her hair flat. She wished there was time to curl it and tease it back up high like it should be, but he was due to be there any moment.

As she stepped out of the bathroom, she saw him standing in front of the café, Don Juan on the leash he'd bought the day before. Wilber was already working his way into her heart. The boys at school had ignored her, but Wilber was pursuing her in a way that was making her head spin. He thought she was special. He'd even told her.

"I'm heading out now, Kelsey!" Bobbi called as she removed her apron and headed for the front door. "I may not be home for dinner!" She saw that Wilber had the same picnic basket over his arm. They wouldn't be able to take ATVs with Don Juan tagging along, but a nice walk sounded good to her.

As soon as she was outside, Wilber took her hand in his, as if he'd held her hand every day of their lives. Her heart skipped a beat as his skin touched hers, and she said a silent prayer that she would never get used to his touch. That every day for the rest of their lives, she would appreciate everything about him, from his ice blue eyes to his huge feet.

"Can we look for Bigfoot today?" she asked softly, trying not to let her feelings show.

He grinned. "I'd love to. Don Juan seems ready."

"Thanks for getting him for me. I'd feel guilty going on a walk without him."

"Do you want to look for Bigfoot or do you want me to show you around the ranch? It's a nice place to live and work."

She wrinkled her brow. "If I vote for seeing the ranch, can I get a raincheck on Bigfoot hunting?"

He nodded. "I'll hunt for Bigfoot anytime you want."

"Then show me the ranch."

He took her over to the stables, introducing her to the man who was in charge of the horses. "Old Bellamy has worked here forever. I can't imagine this ranch without him."

"How long has it been a guest ranch?" she asked.

"My grandmother didn't want to see my grandpa work himself to death, so she turned the ranch hands' house into a hotel. That's where most of the guests stay. And then she decided that it would be nice to have an RV park. My parents added a few cabins. My mom decided she wanted the diner." He pulled her past the stable to an area that she hadn't seen yet. "This is what we call the Old West Town."

"I can see why!" She stared around in surprise. "Do you do anything with these buildings?"

He shook his head. "No, they're really just here for the atmosphere."

"Wouldn't it be nice if the saloon was maybe an ice cream parlor? Or the apothecary shop was a first aid station? You could even turn the mercantile into a combination supply store and a grocery store for the people who stay in the RV park."

He nodded. "I could see that. We could have a pastor who actually performed weddings in the little church. My ancestors first lived in this area of the ranch. We brought in some of the buildings, but that little cabin there? My great-great-grandmother lived there. Legend says that she brought in a mail-order husband. I'd love to find out the real story."

They stopped walking so Don Juan could sniff out just the right place to do his business. "I love that you have stories like that about your family. It sometimes feels like I had no life before the day my dad shot my mother."

He stared at her, shock in his eyes. "Your dad shot your mother?"

She nodded. "He killed her too. He's serving a life sentence. He's eligible for parole in twenty-five years. I hope he rots there."

Wilber pulled her close and kissed her forehead. "I'm sorry life has been so hard for you."

She shrugged. "The harder life is, the stronger I am. That can't be bad."

"I guess not." He continued walking with her, a sad look on his face. "I promise that as soon as you marry me, I won't let anything bad happen to you for the rest of your life."

She laughed. "You can't promise that."

"I can do my very best to make sure that your life is nothing but sunshine and roses after our wedding. How about next week?"

Bobbi laughed, shaking her head. As much as the idea appealed to her, she wanted to make sure she cared for him and not the easy life he could give her. "Let's just get to know each other first. Okay?"

"Okay. You don't know what you're missing, though!"

3

When Wilber came back to the cabin that evening, he no longer seemed angry. He was just sad. It took everything Bobbi had in her not to beg him to forgive her for her words.

She'd finished the dishes and was sitting quietly reading a book Kaya had written about the first Westons who had settled at the ranch. "Are you all right?" she asked softly.

He walked into the living room and sat in a chair perpendicular to her spot on the couch. "I don't know what I am. I thought we were about to celebrate thirty-five years of happy marriage, and you're telling me you're not happy. I can't even figure out what to *think*!"

She closed her eyes for a moment, wanting to make him feel better, but knowing it was past time for how she'd been feeling to be out in the open. "Wilber, I'm not asking for a divorce. I'm asking you to work with me on our marriage. I feel like we've been drifting further and further apart. We're at cross purposes, and I want to feel like we're on the same team again."

"What's it going to take to convince you that I still love

you? And that I'm willing to do what it takes to make our marriage work?"

She bit her lip. She wanted to say, "Let me stay with my grandbabies," but that wasn't fair. Yes, it was the issue that was upsetting her the most at the moment, but there was so much more involved.

"I'm not sure. I do know we need to communicate better. Are you willing to try?"

He nodded, a bit of hope entering his eyes. "I know we can make things work. Don't cancel the celebration yet."

"I won't. The only person who knows about it is Pastor Kevin. Everything else has been kept on the down low. Everyone knows the chapel and kitchen are booked for the day, but no one knows why yet."

"Sounds good." Wilber stood up and moved to sit beside his wife, putting his arm around her. "Tell me about your day."

Bobbi took a deep breath. Asking about her day was a good start. They'd been spending every waking moment in one another's company until they returned to the ranch. It hadn't been a question that had been asked often. "I went and talked to Jaclyn for a little while."

He grinned. "Crazy as ever, I hope?"

"Of course. Then I went and saw Kelsi. I got to hold Willow for a while. The girls are smiling and cooing. I just want to bring them home with me and never let them go."

"Of course you do. I love them too. They're beauties."

"When I got home, I walked down by the lake. It still calms me the way it always did."

"I'm glad." Wilber leaned over and kissed her cheek. "I'm going to leave you to your book. I'm tired, and I have some plans to make."

"What kind of plans?"

He shrugged. "You'll see."

As he left the room, she smiled. He really was a good man, even when she wanted to use an epilator on every square inch of hair on his body.

She thought back to the day he'd walked her around the ranch for the first time, and they'd talked about what they would do with the Old West Town if they'd been running the ranch.

"We need to have the bakery working, too," Wilber told her, her hand still held tightly in his. "And maybe a floral shop. Wouldn't it be nice if a man wanted to propose on the ranch and he could just go get flowers from a shop?"

"Or he could pick wildflowers. I think that's more romantic anyway." Bobbi smiled at the idea of someone picking flowers for her.

"So you'd rather I took my ATV up into the mountains and picked you a bouquet of flowers than I spent an arm and a leg on a dozen roses?"

She nodded. "You can stop at the store and buy me roses anytime. You have to have forethought to go into the mountains for wildflowers."

"I'll keep that in mind. You're going to be different than any girl I've dated, aren't you?"

She frowned at the idea of him dating other women. "You tell me. Am I different?"

He took her hand and brought it to his lips. "You are very different, but in such a good way." He turned and headed a direction she hadn't been yet. She was excited to see all the aspects of her new home. She wasn't sure she'd stay for long, but so far, she couldn't imagine leaving.

As they walked, he pointed out different things. "This path leads to the lake. We have rafting and it's one of the big draws for tourists. Especially in the summer. In the winter, they're here to play in the snow."

She smiled. "I've seen snow a few times, but never much. Southern Oklahoma isn't known for its snowstorms."

He grinned. "We'll go skiing, sledding, and snowmobiling. I promise you're going to love River's End Ranch in the winter. And the fall. And the summer. And the spring. You're just going to love the ranch, because it's so amazing."

"I can't wait to see it in the winter. I can just picture it with a blanket of snow covering it."

"I don't know if an Oklahoma girl is going to be able to handle an Idaho winter. I guess we'll see..."

"Oh, try me. I'm tough." She stopped walking, staring in surprise at a small house along the path. "Who lives there?" She could see bunnies hopping along through the grass.

"Jaclyn."

Bobbi shook her head. "I'm buying her a gnome. She keeps talking about fairies, but I think gnomes are really the brains behind the operation. As soon as I get my first paycheck, that gnome is happening."

"What operation?"

"How am I supposed to know what operation?" She started walking again, pulling him along behind her. Suddenly she was in a huge hurry to see the lake for the first time. "Do people swim in the lake?"

He nodded. "Sure. The temperature isn't exactly warm, so you'll have to get used to it, but people swim there all summer. We're in the process of building a pool as well. That'll be up and running by the beginning of July."

"That sounds like fun. Why have a lake and a pool, though?"

"Different people are looking for different things. Some people don't like swimming in a lake, because there are fish in there as well. And we'll have the pool heated, so there will be a draw to that. Some don't like to swim in pools, because they feel like the chlorine is unnatural. So we try to accommodate as many as we can on the ranch. We're building cabins for the guests to stay in right up against the lake. They will be started as soon as the pool is completed."

"Sounds like you're changing everything around here fast."

He shrugged. "It's kind of a test my parents are putting me through. Dad and I are running the ranch together for a while, but they are leaving all the major decisions to me. He guides me, and tells me if he thinks I'm making a mistake, but at the end of the day, I make the choices. They'll retire before too long, and it'll all be my responsibility."

Bobbi frowned. "Is that what you want?"

"I don't really know. It's something I've always known I'd do as soon as I was old enough. That's how the ranch is run... has been for generations. So I'm doing exactly what I'm supposed to do and passing the test. At least I hope I'm passing. I don't get a lot of feedback from my parents."

"You know, I thought that it would be great to finish school and know where I was going to go and what I was going to do, but I'm not so sure now. I have my whole life in front of me. I have choices. You don't."

"But I have family. My family loves me, and they will guide me for as long as I need to be guided. I won't be left alone to try to figure things out." He stopped on the white sand beach in front of the water. "We had the sand hauled in to make it seem more like an ocean beach."

Bobbi looked around her. The mountains were just behind the lake, and she could see the river that fed into the body of water. "This is beautiful. I could spend all day here just soaking up the atmosphere. What is it that's so calming about water?"

"I have no idea. I know my mom is the same way, though. Anytime she gets stressed out or upset, Dad brings her down here or tells her to take a hot bath. I think that's why a lot of the cabins are being designed to have hot tubs on the back deck. Dad is convinced women are calmer around water."

She wrinkled her nose. "I don't know if I like those generalizations, but it does work for me." She squatted down to rub her hands over the dog's head and neck. "How's it going, Don Juan? Do you love the water too?" Don Juan let out a bark that had her laughing. "I think he understands me!" She glanced up and saw Wilber watching her with a half-grin on his face. "What?"

"Just thinking that you're going to be a fabulous mother. The way you are with that puppy tells me everything I need to know."

She sighed. "You keep trying to move faster than I can handle."

"I know. I'm sorry. I just don't want you to forget that I think you're very special."

She stood, turning to face him. "I have bad blood."

"What's that supposed to mean?"

"My dad came home from work one day to find my mom talking to a man. He shot and killed her. With that kind of violence in my family, how could you even think that I'd be worthy of marrying? Or having kids with? What if my father's violent tendencies are passed down to my kids?"

"Our kids, and I don't believe that. What kind of family did your dad have?"

She shrugged. "I never met his parents. I knew my mother's parents, but they wanted nothing to do with me after my mom died. They said I reminded them of him, and they were done with me."

"That's sad. How could they blame you for what he did?"

"No idea. But I haven't seen them since her funeral, and I lived in the same town as them. I caught a glimpse of Grandma in the grocery store once when I was there with my foster mom, but she turned and ran out of the store. She hated me."

He wrapped his arm around her shoulders, pulling her closer. "I will never hate you. It seems to me that more than anything you want a family—people who will love you forever. Am I right?"

She nodded. "Don Juan will love me forever."

"He will. But so will I. You'll see."

She shrugged, thinking he'd lost his mind, but not having the strength to argue at the moment. "I'm getting hungry. Are you hungry?"

"Sure. There are picnic tables over this way." He walked toward the tables, the dog trotting along behind them. "I had Mom pack the picnic, so I don't even know what we have. I hope you like it."

She shrugged. "I'll eat it whether I like it or not." She'd had no choices in the foster homes where she'd been raised.

He opened the picnic basket and pulled out two paper plates, napkins, and two cans of root beer. "Root beer is kind of a ranch thing. I have a feeling my ancestors made their own, but I have no proof of this."

"Why do you think so then?"

"Because the whole family has always loved root beer. How could our ancestors have been any different?"

Bobbi laughed at his reasoning. "You're silly, you know."

He nodded. "I do know. I'm just glad I can make you laugh. You're too serious most of the time."

"How can you say that when you don't even really know me?"

"I just know. I feel like I've been waiting my entire life for the day you walked onto this ranch. How could I not know little details about you?"

Bobbi took a step closer to him, leaned forward, and rested her forehead against his shoulder. "No matter what happens tomorrow, I'll always treasure this moment with you."

"Tomorrow, I'll spend time trying to convince you we're meant to be together. And you know what I'll do the day after that?" he asked.

She shook her head. "What will you do?"

"The same thing. I will spend the rest of my life proving to you that we can't be whole when we're apart. You were meant for me." He put fried chicken on each of their plates and added a heaping portion of potato salad. "There are brownies for dessert if you eat all your dinner."

She laughed. "I'll do my very best!" Chocolate had always been a weakness of hers, but her foster mother had called it "the "devil's food," so she'd rarely had the opportunity to eat it.

While they ate, Don Juan slept at their feet. She was pleased that he wasn't one of those dogs who would constantly be begging for people food. She'd give him some, of course, because she wanted to treat him, but she'd do it on her terms.

After walking her back to his parents' house that evening, he cupped her face in his hands, leaning down to kiss her goodnight. "I'll see you tomorrow," he told her, leaving her at the door with just a peck on the lips.

She stood and watched him walk away, a hand against her lips. His kiss—well, she had nothing to compare it to, but she knew it had to be the best kiss in all of Idaho. All the world! Kissing him made her skin tingle and her toes curl. She wasn't in love, because no sane person would fall in love with someone they'd only known for forty-eight hours, but she sure was in like. She was very, very much in like!

Bobbi looked down at the book in her hand, wondering how things had changed so very much in thirty-five years. Were they just taking each other for granted? Or was there more to it? She didn't know, but she was determined to find out. She wasn't willing to throw away the life she'd worked so hard to build.

As she slipped into bed beside her husband, she worked hard to transform her thoughts. He was snoring, something that usually annoyed the snot out of her. She would think of his snores as his way of letting her know he was all right. All. Night. Long.

BOBBI WAS UP EARLY THE FOLLOWING MORNING, HAVING agreed to run the diner for the day. The twins had a checkup, and Kelsi wasn't about to let her mother go to the doctor in her place. She quickly dressed, and walked across the ranch's grounds toward the diner. Not much had changed in the place since she'd worked there thirty-five years before.

THE DAY AFTER THEIR FIRST KISS, WILBER HAD COME TO the restaurant for lunch. She was washing dishes when his mother called her. "Time for your lunch break!"

"I'll take it in a few minutes. I want to finish this sinkful." Bobbi had always been very conscientious about her work, but with the Westons giving her a job and a place to stay, she felt like she needed to do as much as she possibly could for them.

Kelsey shook her head. "No, it's time for your lunch break."

Bobbi wanted to continue arguing, but she knew it was no use. Mrs. Weston was very easy on her most of the time. If she wanted her to take a lunch break now instead of later, she would definitely do it.

Untying her apron, she walked out front to one of the

booths. As she started to sit, she heard her name called. "Over here, Bobbi!"

Bobbi turned to see Wilber sitting at a booth, nodding to the other side. She slipped in across from him. "Are you the reason I've been told that I have to take my lunch break now and not later?"

"I can't control my mother! Do you think I can control my *mother*?"

She shook her head with a laugh. "No, I would never presume to think anything like that!"

"Good, because this was all her idea." He picked up her hand and brought it to his lips. "One I wholeheartedly agree with, of course...but her idea."

She tried to pull her hand away, blushing profusely. "You shouldn't do that in such a public place. People will talk."

"They'll say, 'Wilber has good taste. That girl is pretty special.'" He nodded to her menu. "Do you know what you want?"

She shrugged. "I'll just have a cheeseburger."

"Onion rings or fries?"

"Rings sound good."

"Here comes Mom." He ordered for both of them, asking for root beer for them each to drink. As soon as his mother turned away to put their orders in, he pulled a bouquet of wildflowers out from under the table. "I got up before dawn to go up into the mountains and pick them for you. Does this mean I get brownie points?"

She took the flowers from him, burying her face in them. "Thank you."

He grinned, holding her free hand. "I listened to what you said."

"I see that." She frowned down at the flowers. "I have to put them in water so they don't die! I'll be right back." She slipped out of the booth and took them to the back of the diner, putting them in a glass of water. Truthfully, she could have waited longer to put the flowers up, but the tears in her eyes wouldn't have been possible to hide. She didn't know whether he frightened her more than he pleased her. The emotions were probably neck and neck. She was free to pursue a relationship with him, but it felt very wrong to her. But why?

She put the flowers on a windowsill, where she'd be able to see them all day as she worked, before drying her tears and walking back out to the front to sit with Wilber. She kept expecting someone to jump out from behind a bush and tell her that she wasn't good enough for him. She believed it, so it wouldn't be hard to convince her.

"How about I come over tonight and watch a movie with you? My parents have a VCR, and they have more than ten movies to choose from. I'm sure we could find something you haven't seen." He picked her hand up again, saying nothing about her eyes, which she knew must be red. She'd never learned to cry gracefully.

"What about you? Will there be a movie you haven't seen?"

He shook his head. "I've seen them all a dozen times, but that's okay. I want to spend time with you more than I want to watch a movie."

"All right. But only if Don Juan can watch with us. One of the movies they have isn't *Old Yeller*, is it?"

He laughed. "No, but I'm pretty sure they have *The Shaggy DA*."

"Oh, that's definitely a classic doggie movie. Yes, that's the one we'll watch!"

When his mother stopped by the table a minute later with their plates, he said, "We're going to watch something on the VCR tonight."

"That's fine. I think your father is taking me to Riston for dinner anyway."

He narrowed his eyes at his mother for a moment. "Who's going to cook for us, then?"

Kelsey shrugged. "Do you cook, Bobbi?"

"I do. I don't enjoy it a lot, but I can sure do it. I'll cook for us tonight."

Kelsey smiled. "I think that's a fine idea. You're welcome to use anything in the fridge."

Bobbi sighed. How had she been roped into cooking for him? It was only their third time to go out. Surely, he shouldn't be expecting her to cook yet!

4

Bobbi made her way back to the kitchen to make sure Bob was on task. The chef for the diner had his own ways of doing things, and he needed to be watched at times. "What's the special today?"

Bob glanced up from his food preparation. "Dirty rice and jambalaya. I hate making Cajun while Kelsi is here, because she always adds more Cajun seasoning. She makes me crazy with it."

She shrugged. "I know she likes things a little spicier than most people. She hasn't done that since the babies were born, has she?"

"Oh yeah. She said the babies need to learn to tolerate hot foods if they want to be able to hold their heads up in public."

"I never denied she was special." She leaned on the counter, watching as Bob efficiently diced vegetables. "How's Miranda?"

"She's good! And so am I because today is kolache day."

Bobbi stood up straight. "Kolache day? How many and what kinds do you want?" She found a pen and a piece of paper. She'd go get the savory treat for all of the employees of the diner.

After getting the order of everyone there, she opened the front door of the diner to head to the bakery, noting that it was just time for both of the businesses to open. She hurried past the stables, waving at Wyatt as she passed.

"Mom, what's the hurry?" he called.

"It's kolache day at the bakery!"

"I want two ham and cheese!"

She nodded, not breaking her stride. The kolaches disappeared too fast for lollygagging. She got to the bakery, and saw there was already a short line out the front. When she got to the counter, she smiled at Miranda, noting that her belly was starting to grow. There was a definite baby boom there on the ranch, thanks to Jaclyn and her obsession with matchmaking. She gave her order, making casual conversation with the baker.

"That's a lot of kolaches! Are you feeding the whole ranch?" Miranda asked, her eyes twinkling with amusement.

"I'm taking Kelsi's place at the café for today. She has to take the babies to the pediatrician for shots, so she asked me if I'd help out. When Bob told me it was kolache day, I took orders from everyone." Bobbi looked into the display case. "The cinnamon rolls look delicious today. I may need one of those to have for dessert after lunch."

"Works for me." Miranda wrapped up each treat and put them into a white bakery box.

"I'll see you!" Bobbi waved and hurried back toward the café, stopping only at the stable to take Wyatt his kolaches.

Wyatt grinned at her, taking the pastries. "Thanks, Mom."

"I couldn't let my baby starve to death, now could I?"

True to form, Wyatt shook his head and set to eating. With a wave, Bobbi hurried out the door toward the diner.

She was almost there when a figure stepped out from

behind a tall oak tree. She jumped with fright before she realized it was just Wilber. "Good morning!" she called, continuing her walk.

He fell into step beside her. "I brought you something."

She looked at him with a frown, noting the bouquet of wildflowers in his hand. For years, he'd gone the easy route and purchased flowers for special occasions. He hadn't picked wildflowers for her since the twins were born.

"Oh, thank you!" She shoved the bakery box at him and took the flowers, burying her nose in them. "I know just where I'm going to put them."

"Oh? Not on the windowsill this time?"

She laughed. "Well, I'm not on dishwashing duty today." They now had an efficient commercial dishwasher that did the job she'd once done. "I think I'm going to put them on the counter of the café, so I can see them every time I walk in and think about how much my husband cares for me."

He followed her into the café, putting the bakery box on the counter. There were a few customers eating, but the employees descended on the bakery box. "It's kolache day at the bakery," Bobbi told them all as she chose a water glass to put the flowers into.

One of the deputy sheriffs, Seth, was there, and he groaned. "I'm going to have to hightail it over to the bakery as soon as I finish my breakfast. Sheriff will never forgive me if I don't bring him a kolache. They're his favorite."

"They're everyone's favorite," Bob said as he came from the kitchen to grab two of the pastries for himself.

Seth frowned at Bob. "I think it's time you told your wife to start making them every day. This twice a week thing is for the birds."

"If she had time she'd do them every day, but they're very labor-intensive. If you want to go and volunteer your time every morning, I bet she'd make them." Bob hurried back to the kitchen with his kolaches in hand, knowing the other man wouldn't take him up on the plan he'd made.

Bobbi looked over at Wilber, who was watching the byplay. "Maybe it's time for us to hire another baker to help Miranda. If she can't make the food that's most in demand *every* morning, then we're missing out on income." He waved to his wife. "I'm going to go and get some kolaches and then talk to Wade. Maybe he's got some reason that I can't comprehend to explain why he hasn't hired someone to help her full-time."

As he left, Bobbi frowned. He was back in work mode, so she was forgotten. It was the way of things, but it wasn't something she liked. She loved the ranch every bit as much as he did, but she loved her family more. She knew he did too, but he didn't always show things the same way.

As she waited tables, her mind drifted back again.

Wilber arrived just at the time he'd said he would. She added punctuality to her mental list of positive points.

"I'm in the kitchen!" she called when he yelled out, looking for her. She'd made a simple meal—one she'd made a thousand times. Her foster mother had expected her to cook three nights a week. She'd said that every girl should know how to cook, so she'd be a proper wife.

Bobbi had always doubted she'd be a wife because she didn't think any man would want her, but she had done as she was told. She'd always strived to be the foster child who caused the least amount of trouble.

Wilber walked into the kitchen and found her serving up two plates of spaghetti with garlic bread. He took the plates from her hands and placed them on the kitchen table before gripping her waist and pulling her to him for a kiss. "I didn't think I'd ever get to do that again. It feels like it's been years since I've kissed you!"

She shook her head, ignoring the tingling in her lips.

"We've known each other for three days, and it feels like years since you've kissed me? You have a warped sense of time, Wilber Weston."

He just grinned, leaning down to pat Don Juan on the head. If she wasn't working, the puppy was at her side. "Dinner smells delicious."

"I hope it tastes good." Bobbi was being modest. She knew she was a good cook, but she hated doing it so much. She wished she was more like his mother, who seemed to love being in the kitchen.

"I'm sure it will." He sat down, picking up his fork. "Who taught you to cook?"

"My foster mother. The last one. I had four between the ages of eight and ten. No one wanted the child of a murderer in their home. So they kept shoving me off to the next home."

"The last one didn't mind though?"

She shook her head. "She was sure she could *fix* me." She'd used religion as her weapon of choice, but Bobbi didn't tell him that. It was enough for him to know she'd been with the woman for eight years. Maybe someday she'd tell him all about the places she'd lived, but for now, she didn't want him to look at her with pity or fear in his eyes.

After the meal, they did the dishes together, which thrilled her. "My foster brothers were never expected to help with dishes. It was the girls' job."

"Well, I think men and women should share chores equally."

"Are you still going to feel that way after thirty years of marriage?" she asked, her eyes dancing merrily.

"No promises, but I hope I will."

They watched the Disney movie together, laughing at the antics of the man changing into a dog. Don Juan seemed to be paying attention at times, but usually he had his head resting on Bobbi's knee. She was his favorite human, after all.

At the end of the night, she walked him to the door. It was strange for her, knowing she was living in his parents' house while he lived elsewhere, but that was the situation they were in. This time she reached out to him, wrapping her arms around his neck for his kiss. She found his kisses to be better than any chocolate she'd ever had, and that was saying a lot.

He leaned down and brushed his lips against hers gently, and then more firmly. "I'll see you tomorrow. May I come to have lunch with you?"

She nodded. "I'd like that a lot." She walked back to her small room, Don Juan following alongside her. She closed her bedroom door and turned on the radio, needing to lose herself in the music. She had always loved music, and would have liked to learn an instrument, but it cost too much for just a foster child. Of course the birth children of her foster parents had been allowed to play anything they wanted, but it was forbidden to her.

She danced to the song on the radio, feeling as if she was doing something slightly wicked. Dancing had been forbidden to her as well. As the song ended, she heard the announcer's voice. "There's been a prison break in Oklahoma. Please be on the lookout for..." She didn't hear the rest—she'd frozen in place. Her father had tried to write letters to her over the years, but she'd returned them all unopened.

She walked into the bathroom and stood under the shower spray, allowing the water to wash over her, not realizing until she was getting out that she'd forgotten to remove her clothes. Silently, Bobbi prayed, "Please, God, don't let it be my father who has escaped. I couldn't bear to see him."

Bobbi shook her head, refusing to think about her father. He'd been in prison for more than forty years, and she needed to forget him. She slid two specials onto a table in front of two men she didn't know. "If you need anything else, be sure to let me know. My name is Bobbi."

She turned and walked back toward the kitchen, pestering Bob for her next order. Keeping her mind off her father was always best. He was due to be out soon, she knew. She couldn't remember exactly when.

As she was finishing up her shift, she spotted Dani walking toward her. "Mom, you have a letter."

Bobbi took the letter and slipped it into her pocket, knowing that time with her older daughter was more important than any letter that could be found. "How's my girl?"

Dani pushed her hair out of her eyes. "I'm good. Happy. You did the right thing sending Travis to me. He's the perfect husband for me."

"I'm glad. I heard something about the two of you racing four-wheelers through the mountain paths. Is that true?"

Dani laughed. "I can neither confirm nor deny this rumor..."

"Just be careful. I only have two daughters, and I don't want to lose one of them!"

"But if I was Wyatt?"

"I don't want to lose him. He's good with the horses. Maybe Will..."

Dani shook her head. "Your heart would break into a million pieces if you lost any of us, and you know it."

"Of course it would. Just don't tell your brothers that, would you?"

"Too late, Mom. We already know how much you love us. You wouldn't be so hard on us otherwise."

Bobbi smiled at that. "That's all your father. I'm just the unfortunate messenger at times." She leaned toward Dani, ready to impart a secret. She didn't know why she felt the need to tell her anything, but she was feeling very nostalgic.

"Your father was forced to jump through hoops to see if he was ready to take over the ranch thirty-five years ago. His tests lasted three years, if I remember correctly. He hated it as much as you and your brothers and sister do."

"Really?" Dani asked, obviously surprised.

"Really. Whose turn is it to cook this Sunday?"

"Kelsi's. Are you coming?"

"It's a family dinner. Why wouldn't I come? Am I not family?"

"Well, you don't always, so I was just wondering."

Bobbi grinned, hugging her daughter. "We'll be there. Tell Kelsi to chop up a few more jalapeno peppers." As Dani ran off, Bobbi dug the letter out of her pocket, frowning when she saw the familiar address. It was from the prison. Again.

Tucking it back into her pocket, she walked the rest of the way to the cabin she was sharing with Wilber. When she walked in, she saw four different vases around the room, each filled with wildflowers, and a smile tilted her lips. Her husband was courting her, and she liked it. More than she probably should.

She walked to the couch and sat down, removing the letter from her pocket again. She knew she should read it. She'd refused every letter for forty-three years. It was time she read something he sent her.

She slid her finger under the flap of the envelope and took out the single sheet of paper. She didn't want to read it, and she almost put it back in unread, but it was time.

Dear Roberta,

I have written you more times than I can count over the years, hoping you will forgive me. Your mother is the only woman I have ever loved, and what I did was inexcusable. I had been drinking, but that's no reason for my behavior. I miss you every day, and I hope you'll agree to see me when I get out of prison at the end of the month. It would mean the world to me.

FOREVER FAMILY

I know you have six children, because I keep up with your life as best I can using the prison library. I would like to meet my grandchildren. Please let me be a part of your life.

Your father.

Bobbi shuddered, stuffing the letter back into the envelope. Of course she wasn't going to let a murderer be around her children. She'd done everything she could to protect them over the years, and she wasn't going to invite him into her home.

She sat staring into space, thinking about the prison break all those years ago. It hadn't taken long for the police to find her and interview her. She had used her social security number when she'd started working for the ranch, after all.

The previous sheriff had been nothing like her son-in-law, Shane Clapper. He'd been an older man with a beer belly who'd looked at her as if she was guilty when he'd walked into the diner to talk to her.

"Are you Bobbi Jackson? Daughter of Reginald Jackson?"

Bobbi nodded. "I am. Could we talk about this in private please?"

She knew they were there about her father escaping, and she knew she was innocent of any wrongdoing. So why was she shaking so badly?

The sheriff, Steve Jameson, had led her outside to stand beside the café. She knew the customers and other employees were watching her, but she was powerless to do anything about it. "How can I help you, sheriff?"

"Are you aware that your father has escaped from a maximum-security prison in Oklahoma?"

Bobbi shook her head. "I haven't seen or spoken to my father since before his trial. I was taken from him as soon as it was determined that he'd murdered my mother."

"Are you saying your father has never written to you? In ten years?"

She took a deep breath. "He's written to me repeatedly. I have returned the letters unopened. Why would I want to talk to the man who murdered my mother?" Why could people not understand why she wouldn't have anything to do with the man?

"So he hasn't come to see you since his escape?"

She shook her head. "No, sir, he hasn't. As far as I know, he thinks I'm still in Oklahoma. I came here to lose the stigma of being the girl whose father was a murderer. I want nothing to do with him."

"Do you have any idea where your father would go?"

She shook her head. "None."

"What did he like to do before his incarceration?"

"I was eight years old the last time I saw him. I remember he liked to drink, play pool, and he liked to push me on the swing in our backyard." As she said the words, her heart ached. As long as she could think of him as the man who'd killed her mother, she was fine. When she had to think of him as her daddy, it hurt beyond belief.

"Do you know which bar he liked to drink at?"

"No, sir. I have no idea."

"Which pool hall he frequented?"

Bobbi shook her head. "I really don't remember at all."

"Will you get in touch with the sheriff's department if he contacts you?"

"Yes, of course I will."

The sheriff had shaken her hand and walked away, leaving her standing there with everyone watching out the window of the café. She wanted to pack her things and leave right there and then, but she couldn't. She had already become attached to Kelsey Weston, and her feelings for Wilber were stronger than she'd imagined possible after a four-day acquaintance.

So instead of going to the house where she was staying to pack her things, she walked right toward the front door of the café, ignored all the people gaping at her, and walked back to the kitchen to work on the dishes.

Kelsey had come to the back and put her hand on her shoulder. "Are you all right?"

Bobbi nodded, the tears stinging her eyes. If Kelsey had been accusatory, she would have been able to hold up so much easier, but there was sympathy in the older woman's voice. "I'm fine. My father escaped from prison, so they're questioning me. They want me to let them know if he tries to contact me."

"Has he?"

Bobbi shook her head. "No, not since I've been here. He sent me letters every week when I was in Oklahoma."

"What did he say in them?"

"No idea. I sent them all back unopened. I had no desire to hear from him."

Kelsey studied her for a moment. "I'm here if you need to talk. God never blessed me with a daughter, but I've come to think of you as one."

Bobbi stared at the older woman with surprise on her face. "In four days? My foster mother had me for eight years, and I was never more than a burden to her."

"Yes, in four days. You're a remarkable young lady. Anyone else would have run, but you came back in here and got right back to work."

"I thought about running," Bobbi whispered.

"Why didn't you?" Kelsey asked.

"Because I feel like I'm part of a family for the first time in ten years. I can't leave." Bobbi turned to Kelsey and buried her face in the older woman's shoulder, the tears soaking Kelsey's shirt.

"You *are* a part of our family now. We want you to stay forever—whether you continue to have a relationship with Wilber or not."

Bobbi brushed the tears from her eyes as she looked down at the letter in her hand. How could he want to come back into her life after all this time? It had been forty-five years since she'd seen him. How could he think she'd want anything to do with him?

Wilber walked into the house to see her crying on the sofa, and she handed him the letter, saying nothing. She didn't need to. After thirty-five years of marriage, he knew how she felt about her father, though they'd seldom discussed him over the years. It was a subject she didn't talk about.

5

Wilber spent the entire day trying to think of ways he could show his wife that she was still the woman he loved beyond words or his wildest imagination. He went into town and found her a necklace that he knew she'd been eyeing, and he'd stopped to get dinner because she'd worked in the café all day. He knew she hated to cook anyway.

He opened the door to the cabin, expecting to arrive just before Bobbi did, and instead found her sitting on the couch, her head in her hands—sobbing. He set the Chinese take-out on the counter and rushed over to the couch, sitting beside her and gathering her close. "What is it?"

Bobbi couldn't speak, so she simply handed him the letter.

Wilber felt a ball of pain forming in his throat. "What do you want to do?" He remembered the day all those years ago when her father had escaped from prison. It hadn't been pretty. His mother had sent her home from work early, telling her to take a nap. Then she'd found someone to track him down where he was working with his father.

He'd been with his father on horseback, scouting out a

place for a new ski lift to be put in, when he received a note from his mother.

As soon as he read the note, he panicked. "I need to go talk to Bobbi."

His father frowned. "This ranch is your first love. Not some girl who came in on the latest bus and could leave any minute."

Wilber's eyes had met his father's. "I've always known this ranch was my future, but I'll tell you now that she's more important to me than this land. She's been the most important thing in my life since I laid eyes on her. If you can't understand that, I'm not the man to run this ranch for you." With that he pulled the reins of his horse to one side and started down the mountain.

By the time he'd gotten to the house, his heart was in his throat. He rushed through the house, calling her name. When he got to her bedroom door, he knocked, though he wanted to just rush in and hold her. She needed him, and he'd been off working. She came first, and she always would. He *had* to show her that.

"Come in." Her voice was soft, and he could tell she'd been crying.

He opened the door and walked in. She was lying on her stomach on the bed, sobbing uncontrollably. He sat on the bed beside her, his hand stroking her back and her hair, which had come out of the ponytail she wore for work. "Mom sent me a message that you needed me. Are you all right?"

She sat up, shaking her head. "I think I need to move on. I can't stay here, suspected by the police. I've done nothing wrong!"

"And that's exactly why you *will* stay here. You've done nothing, and you need to be with people who know that. People who care about you."

She leaned into him, and he let his arms close around her.

He didn't let himself worry about the situation they were in—alone, on her bed—but just tried to take the pain away. "I don't want your parents to run into trouble," she finally said, swiping the tears off her face. "They've been so kind to me."

"Running will do nothing good. I'd have to go with you, and then my parents would have to find another son to run the ranch..."

She laughed softly. "You can't go with me. Your whole life is here."

He cupped her face in his hands. "I don't think you understand. My whole life is *you*."

"What if he comes here looking for me?"

He cocked his head to one side, studying her face. "Are you worried he'll hurt you?"

She shook her head adamantly. "No. Not at all. He's never hurt me in any way."

"Then what would it hurt to stay here? Surely you've had contact with him over the years."

"I haven't. Not at all. He wrote me every week while I was still in my foster home, but I returned all letters unopened."

He frowned. "Why do you think he's broken out, then?"

She shrugged. "Why does anyone break out of prison? He doesn't look good in orange, and it's not where he wants to be? I've heard it's not exactly a vacation."

"You don't think there's more to it than that?"

"Like what?"

"Maybe he's worried about you. Is that possible? He doesn't know where you are, now that you're not in a foster home anymore. He could be looking for you to make sure you're all right."

"I guess..."

"Are you sure he killed your mother?"

She slowly nodded. "I was in my bedroom. Mom was in the living room talking to the pastor. He was a new pastor, and Dad never went to church, so he didn't know him. When Dad got home, he was drunk, and he went for the pastor's throat. Mom tried to stop him and he backhanded her, sending her flying into the wall. She fell and hit her head." Taking a deep breath, she said, "The pastor testified against him, and he confessed. They called it second degree murder."

He pursed his lips. "Sounds like it's more manslaughter, but that's neither here nor there. Do you have any desire to see him?"

The tears started flowing again. She had visions of him picking her up and swinging her around. Of him pushing her on the swing and calling her Bobbita. "No. He killed my mother."

"All right. What do you want to do?"

"What do you mean? What *can* I do?"

"Do you want to go? Because I can pack what I need and be ready within the hour. Or are you going to stay here and stick it out. Here, where you have a family."

She sniffled. "A forever family? That's what I've wanted since the day my mom died. A forever family."

"If you want us forever, then you'll have us. Mom has decided you're the daughter she always wanted, and it has nothing to do with your relationship with me. She's keeping you."

Bobbi smiled a little, but the tears were still flowing. "I'm going to stay here. If he finds me, he won't hurt me. I know he won't."

He pulled her close, her head coming to rest on his shoulder. "I'm glad. I didn't want to leave."

"Thank you!"

Wilber shook his head and realized where he was as he frowned down at the letter in his hands. "How do you want to handle it?" He knew she'd gotten hundreds of letters over the years, but to his knowledge, this was the first one she'd opened.

She shrugged. "I really have no idea. It's been forty-five years since I've seen him. Thirty-five since I've heard his voice. I don't know what to think or feel. It's like I'm the confused little girl who lost her mother all over again."

"But you're not. You're a successful woman who has raised six pretty darned awesome kids—seven including Jess. You're strong and confident. He can't take that away from you."

She sniffled again. "I'm just so torn. Am I being unforgiving? He is my father. How am I supposed to forgive him, though? Our kids never knew their grandmother. Well, they knew their Grandma Kelsey, who was pretty awesome, but not my mom. He's also in his seventies. He's alone in the world with no one. And I won't speak to him? His own flesh and blood?"

"Maybe we should ask the kids if they want to meet him. Are we going to the family dinner on Sunday? That would be a good place to bring it up."

She sighed. "They all know. But it's one thing to know your grandfather killed your grandmother and another to come face to face with said grandfather. I just don't know the right thing to do. And Kelsi has those two precious babies. Can I let him be around them?"

Wilber shrugged. "If you meet him with our boys around, there would be no danger. We have four strong sons. Two strong sons-in-law. Jake would be there. Nothing would happen to you or those babies. Nothing."

She tilted her head to the side and thought about it for a moment. "That's true. And we can ask Shane to bring his gun and his deputies if we're that worried about it."

"You could invite him to come to our thirty-fifth anniversary celebration and vow renewal."

She frowned at him. "You know that hasn't been decided yet!"

"It's about to be. Wait 'til you see what I brought you!" He kissed her forehead. "Close your eyes."

Bobbi laughed, even as she obeyed. Her husband had spent more than half of her life bringing her surprises. How could she stay mad at him?

A moment later, he picked up her hand and put something warm in it. She looked down and laughed. "Chinese takeout. How did you know I wasn't going to be up to cooking tonight?"

"I know my wife!" He took the necklace box and laid it on the couch beside her. "You don't get the surprise until you eat all your supper."

She grinned, remembering what he'd said to her at their first picnic. "All we need is Don Juan here to make things perfect."

"I haven't thought about Don Juan in forever. What made you think of him?"

She shrugged. "I've been thinking a lot about my first days on the ranch lately. I miss your mom and Don Juan the most."

He nodded. "I miss them both too. Kelsi seems to be just like her other than the eyes."

"Yeah, she does."

As they ate, Bobbi kept looking at the letter, which was lying on the coffee table. "I'm not sure I should have read that letter."

"I think you're wrong. You did the right thing."

She bit her lip. "Maybe. I do think I'm going to talk to the kids about it on Sunday. I think they should have a say in what we decide."

"Promise me the final decision will still be yours."

"It will be. They don't know him, and I do." She frowned. "Well, I did."

The following morning, Bobbi decided she needed to make another trip over to see Jaclyn. Maybe she could talk out what had happened with the older woman and let her give an opinion. She already knew, so why not?

As she walked, she thought about her first visit to the little house at the edge of the RV camp. She'd been given Wednesday off, because Kelsey thought she needed time to think about what was going on with her father.

First thing that morning, a letter had been hand-delivered to her as she ate breakfast.

Dear Miss Jackson,

I would like to request the honor of your presence for tea and snickerdoodles this afternoon. The fairies would like to get a closer look at you. Please arrive at two. Thank you.

Jaclyn Hardy

She was nervous about seeing the crazy woman, but Kelsey assured her she'd be fine. Even Wilber had told her that she'd been an honorary aunt to him his entire life. She refused to be frightened.

As she wandered through the gate and into the yard with the bunnies hopping everywhere, Jaclyn stepped onto her porch, her hand over her eyes. "It's about time! The fairies are getting antsy!"

"Do you always talk to fairies, Miss Hardy?"

"Oh, call me Jaclyn. Miss Hardy makes me seem like an old woman sitting on a porch and knitting shawls for my bunnies. And no, I don't always talk to fairies. In fact, they just started talking to me a few days before you arrived. They told me you were coming, and that you'd be in need of my help. So? How can I help you?"

"I...don't know. I came only because of your invitation."

"Well, then it sounds like the fairies need to be more forthcoming!"

Bobbi looked down at the paper bag she held in her

hands. She'd almost forgotten, and that wouldn't be right after begging Wilber to take her on an errand in town during his lunch hour. "I brought you something."

Jaclyn put her hand over her chest in surprise. "You did? Well, I don't have anything for you!"

"That's all right." Bobbi felt like she was on firmer ground now, and she was so glad she'd gotten the gift. It had taken all the tips she'd earned from the few tables she'd waited while the waitresses were on break, but that was all right. It was something special, and she knew it would suit Jaclyn perfectly.

"Well, come in and I'll open it while I'm sitting. That will be better, right?"

Bobbi had no answer for that, so she walked into the house, looking around for a place to sit. "Exactly how many bunnies do you have?"

"Only twelve. I had four, but…you know how bunnies are. Just scoop one up and you can hold it or set it on the floor."

Bobbi was suddenly glad she'd decided to leave Don Juan at home. He would have loved the walk, but he would have wanted to chase the bunnies. It would have been a fun new game for him, but she was certain Jaclyn wouldn't approve. She scooped a bunny out of the chair and planted her bottom in it, stroking the bunny's head.

Jaclyn opened the paper sack and squealed with surprise. "It's a gnome! For my yard? He's perfect. I shall call him George, and he shall reign over the fairies with an iron fist!" She leaned toward the gnome, as if she was listening. "What's that? The gnomes and the fairies are natural enemies? Life is about to get interesting around here, I see!"

"I'm sorry I didn't wrap it. There was no time."

"It's perfect. George isn't one who needs frou-frou wrapping paper. He's content just the way he is." Jaclyn sighed happily. "I can't wait to put him in my yard. Maybe I'll start an entire gnome village!"

"I think that would be very wise," Bobbi said, struggling to keep her face straight.

"So you really don't know why the fairies wanted me to help you? Nothing bad is going on in your life?" Jaclyn's eyes narrowed at Bobbi, obviously thinking she was holding something back from her.

Bobbi bit her lip, wondering how much she should tell the older woman. Finally, she decided to spill it all. Why not? The whole ranch would soon know that her father was an escaped con. She spilled the story quickly and emotionlessly. She didn't want Jaclyn to realize just how upset she was over the whole thing.

"So, has your father called you?"

Bobbi shook her head. "Not yet. I think he will, though."

"How do you feel about seeing him?"

"I don't know. As my father, I want to see him, of course. As my mother's murderer, it's harder to want to see him." Bobbi raised her hands, as if confused.

"I'm not sure that's why the fairies wanted you to come over. I think you're here to talk about your feelings for Wilber."

"Wilber?" Bobbi blushed profusely. "What exactly am I supposed to say?" How could she admit feelings she had to this woman when she hadn't even admitted them to herself?

"How do you feel? I know he saw you and knew he'd marry you, but how do you feel about him?" Jaclyn leaned forward, studying her face.

Bobbi took a deep breath. "He's a very kind man, and I like him a great deal."

"Enough to marry him?"

"Having known him for precisely five days, that's hard to answer. Maybe once I've known him for a week, I'll have a better handle on my feelings." Even Bobbi was surprised by the sarcasm that dripped from her words. Her foster mother had been determined to make certain she never used that tone of voice again. "I'm sorry. That was rude."

Jaclyn simply laughed. "Not rude at all. When you've only known a man for a week and people keep bugging you about your feelings for him, sarcasm is definitely called for! I approve."

Bobbi smiled. "I'm glad you do." She shrugged. "I like him a lot. I've never had a boyfriend before, and he's a very sweet man to be my first."

"And last. I think the fairies are pushing for the two of you to marry. They approve of you together."

"Did they tell you that?" Bobbi asked.

"Honestly, the fairies talking to me is very new. They told me that you were about to come to the ranch and that you would marry Wilber. They said the two of you are destined to be together, but you would perceive obstacles before you that you didn't need to worry about. So stop worrying about them."

"I can't marry a man while my father is on the loose. It wouldn't *feel* right." Bobbi knew she was looking for reasons not to marry quite yet. As much as she cared about Wilber, it didn't feel like it was time.

"Would it feel wrong, though?" Jaclyn asked.

"I don't know. Maybe." Bobbi felt as if Jaclyn's role in life was to confuse her.

Jaclyn cocked her head to one side. "The fairies say he'll be back in prison tomorrow. Will that make you feel better about everything?"

"My father being in prison doesn't make me feel good. How could it?"

"I guess that makes sense." Jaclyn looked down. "Oh, I forgot to offer you tea and snickerdoodles. Do you like snickerdoodles? They're the only cookie I bake, but I bake them like a champ."

"I think so. I don't remember ever having them." There had been few treats in Bobbi's life for the past ten years.

"Well, try one!" Jaclyn peered at her anxiously, making Bobbi feel a bit like a bug in a glass jar.

Bobbi took a small plate and added one of the cookies to it, also pouring herself a cup of the tea. She took a bite of the cookie and closed her eyes, smiling big. "They're delicious."

Jaclyn sat back happily. "I told the fairies that snickerdoodles would be good and you didn't need chocolate chip. They were very fussy about it though. Do fairies talk to people everywhere you go?"

"If they do, no one has ever mentioned it to me before. Do you think they'll stop talking to you? Or will they continue?" Bobbi didn't believe in fairies, but it was so fun to play along with the game the older woman was playing. Surely it wouldn't hurt anything for her to pretend fairies were real.

"Oh, I think now that they've opened their big mouths, they'll never be able to close them. I don't mind though. It's kind of nice to have the company."

Bobbi shook her head, stopping in front of the house. Over the years, she and Jaclyn had become very close, and she'd grown used to the fairy talk. She'd even spent hours consoling Jaclyn over the death of George.

Sure enough, as she walked up to the house, Jaclyn stuck her head out. "The fairies said you were coming. I have tea and snickerdoodles. Though the fairies still insist I should be baking chocolate chip cookies for you."

"The fairies are silly." Bobbi didn't wait for an invitation into the house, knowing she was welcome. They'd been friends for too long for her to suspect anything else at all.

Once she was inside, Bobbi shooed a couple of bunnies from her favorite chair, determined that she would not have to deal with them. As much as she loved bunnies, what she wanted to talk about was serious, and not meant to be filled with animals.

She waited while Jaclyn set everything just so and poured her a cup of tea. "I thought you needed something special today, so I made chamomile." Jaclyn flinched. "Okay! The *fairies* insisted on chamomile."

"Chamomile is perfect," Bobbi said, accepting the cup. "And as much as I love your snickerdoodles, the fairies were right about the cookies. I need all the chocolate I can get my hands on at the moment."

Jaclyn studied her over the rim of her own cup. "Tell me everything."

6

Bobbi took a deep breath, trying to decide where to start. "Do you remember when I told you about my father?"

Jaclyn nodded slowly. "He'd just escaped from prison, and you were trying to decide what to do."

"He's getting out at the end of the month. He knows where I am, and he wants a relationship with me and his grandchildren." Bobbi bit into the cookie, wishing it would magically transform itself into chocolate.

"Wow. What are you going to do?"

Bobbi shrugged. "I don't know! We've decided to talk to the kids about it on Sunday at the family dinner. We think they have a right to help us decide. He's their last living grandparent, after all."

"Do they know about him?"

"They know their grandfather killed their grandmother, and he's been in prison since I was a child. Nothing more." What more was there to say? If she thought about it, that covered all they really needed to know.

"That's a tough situation," Jaclyn said, shaking her head.

"Are you hoping for help from the fairies? They only seem to have opinions on people's love lives. They told me you and Wilber are doing a bit better."

"There's nothing like a crisis to help us see eye-to-eye." Bobbi sighed, running her fingers through her hair. It was still as blond as it had been in the eighties, but now she helped it with regular salon appointments. "And no, I'm not looking for help from the fairies. I thought maybe my friend Jaclyn might have an opinion."

Jaclyn looked almost afraid to give her advice. "I only pass on what the fairies say. You know I don't give advice."

Bobbi shrugged. "It was worth a try. This is one of those days when I really wish I had Kelsey around to talk to. She always made me feel like everything was better." She knew the good relationship she'd had with her mother-in-law wasn't considered normal by most people, but she'd truly appreciated the older woman's advice on everything from home décor to cooking.

Jaclyn frowned. "You think you feel better after talking to her? She was my closest friend for over fifty-five years. Not having her around anymore is hard every single day."

Bobbi nodded. "For me too. I know I'm supposed to hate my mother-in-law, but I never could. She was too loving."

"She loved you too. She always called you her daughter-in-love, and said you stole her heart the first day you walked on the ranch. Knowing you and Wilber are having problems would make her roll over in her grave."

"We're working through them. I promise. He's always been my staunchest supporter." Bobbi felt badly for even being annoyed with him and questioning their relationship, because he had always been very good to her. Well, except for lately, of course.

"You don't need advice from me, Bobbi. You know just what to do. Talk to your children, get their feelings, and then make a decision. If you don't think he's dangerous, maybe it's time for you to forgive him."

"How do you forgive a man for killing your mother and changing the course of your life?"

"If he hadn't killed her, do you think you'd be sitting here talking to me today? Do you think you'd have married Wilber and been happy?"

Bobbi shrugged. She truly didn't know, but it was something to think about. She had six children that she loved more than her own life, as well as a niece she'd raised and loved as one of her own. The grandbabies were starting to roll in, and the joy she got from them was indescribable. Could she really keep her father from experiencing the same joy?

After leaving Jaclyn's house, she walked over toward the spa. There was rarely an opening without an appointment, but she was hoping she could get in today. She desperately needed a massage—one where she did no talking and she just lay there and let her therapist relax her.

As she walked, she thought about her father's call the day after she'd gone to see Jaclyn. She'd just returned to the ranch house after her day of work when the phone rang. Kelsey had called her. "It's a man. The police are ready to trace the call. Can you keep him on the line?"

Bobbi shuddered. How had her life been reduced to being bait for her father? She didn't know, but she would do what was right.

"Hello?"

"Bobbi, are you okay?" It was definitely her father, and he sounded frantic. She had no desire to talk to him, but she had to. She had to do what was right, to help the police get him back into custody.

"I'm fine, Dad." She nodded at Kelsey who slipped into the office to make a call to the police. "I'm living on a ranch here in Idaho, and if God made a more beautiful place on this earth, I've yet to see it."

"Well, it's not like you've been a lot of places. I've been really worried about you. They told me you left your foster home, but you'd not left a forwarding address. I've been searching for you since I got the news. I had to break out so I could find you. I've known how for a while, but I didn't *need* to."

"I see." She looked over at Kelsey, who gave her a thumbs up. "Where are you, Dad?"

"I'm staying in a small town near the prison, sleeping in the woods. I had to do research to find you. Research I couldn't have done from prison. I broke into someone's house to use their phone. As soon as the police arrive, I'll give myself up."

Bobbi blinked. "What do you mean?" He knew they were tracing the call? How?

"I knew I'd be caught as soon as I called you. You've always been a rule follower, and someone who would do what she thought was right, even if it meant giving up her own father. It's okay. I'm sure they'll be here soon."

She stood there frozen, unsure what to say. "You knew?"

"I did. I love you just the way you are, Bobbi. I'll do extra time for this, but at least I know you're safe."

She felt the tears streaming down her face. He couldn't understand as much as he said he did. The phone was taken from her, and Wilber pulled her against him. "They've got him."

She could hear the sirens through the phone line even as he put the phone back on the cradle. "Please tell me I did the right thing."

"Of course you did! You did the only thing you could do."

"But he's my *dad*." It was the first time she'd thought of

him as her father in years. He'd always just been her mother's killer.

"I know, sweetheart. I know."

She clung to him, unsure if she'd done the right thing or not. It was the only contact she'd had with her father in ten years, and she didn't plan to have more contact with him anytime soon. Maybe she should, but he was a killer.

"Let's take Don Juan for a walk," he suggested, kissing her forehead. "I think you need to clear your head before supper."

"You're probably right." She went to her room, where Don Juan was sleeping on her bed. She'd never known a dog could sleep quite so much. She attached his leash, and went out into the living room where Wilber was waiting, talking to his mom in low tones.

"You ready?" he asked as he saw her.

She nodded. "Let's go."

"I'll have her back in an hour or two, Mom."

"Good. She has to be up very early for work in the morning."

Bobbi smiled at Kelsey, happy that she still had a job. It wouldn't have been hard for Kelsey to tell her that it wasn't working out because of the drama she brought to the ranch.

As they walked, Wilber talked to her, getting her mind off her father. "Do you want to go down by the lake?"

She laughed softly. "So it can calm me down, because I'm a woman?"

"I didn't say that..."

"You didn't need to. I remember your theories." She sighed. "As it happens, a walk down by the lake sounds absolutely lovely. I can't think of a place I'd rather go."

He grinned. "I'm not saying a word."

"You'd better not. I have awfully sharp elbows, and you just might get one in your side if you do."

He laughed. "I can't believe you're threatening me when I'm taking you for a walk so you'll feel better…"

"I guess I'm just mean like that."

"Obviously. It's a good thing I fell in love with you at first sight, or I might just be afraid of you right about now."

She shook her head. "You didn't fall in love with me at first sight. I don't even believe in love at first sight. I think you need to get to know someone before you can love them."

"You do, huh? So you think love is more of a choice than it is an emotion you feel?"

"I wouldn't go that far. I mean, I know I can choose to love people and not hate them, but it's more than that. I think that as you get to know someone, that's when you fall in love…or don't, as the case may be."

"Well, that's not how it happened for me. I took one look at you, and I knew I was going to spend the rest of my life with you. It came on like a blinding flash."

"Jaclyn would say it was the fairies. She says they told her we were meant to be together. I tried to talk to her about my troubles with my father, but she told me the fairies had only told her about you. Not my dad."

He laughed. "I love that crazy woman!"

She grinned. "I think she's growing on me. I was a little afraid of her at first, because every time she saw me, she was mumbling about fairies, but she invited me over for tea and snickerdoodles yesterday. I don't think I've ever had a snickerdoodle, and while I will always prefer chocolate chip, the snickerdoodles were very good!"

He frowned. "She hasn't made me snickerdoodles since I was a boy. I think I need to go visit Jaclyn for my fair share of cookies."

"Be my guest. She loved the gnome, by the way. Said she's naming him George."

"I guess George is as good a name for a gnome as anything. I wonder if the fairies have names."

"You're going to have to ask her that. I'm not going to talk about the fairies any more than absolutely necessary."

He frowned. "I wonder if we're going to be required to invite the fairies when we marry. I have no idea what the protocol is when fairies are instrumental in your relationship."

"No idea. Maybe you should ask your mother. Better yet, ask your dad. I'm sure he'll have an opinion."

"I can just picture my dad's face if I ask him that. And you didn't argue this time when I told you we were getting married. I'm making progress!"

She laughed. "I'm not sure what to say to you anymore. I've argued until my face is blue, and you still say that we're getting married. What's a girl to do?"

"Marry me?"

"We'll see."

"You're still waiting for the perfect proposal, aren't you?"

"I've known you six days. I'm not waiting for any proposal, perfect or not."

He stopped walking and turned to her. "I want you to know that even if I seem flippant about it, I'm very serious. I want to spend the rest of my life with you, living on this ranch and raising babies. How many kids do you want?"

She shrugged. "Maybe a half dozen or so. All girls."

"Girls? What would we do with a houseful of girls? You can have two girls, but I want the rest to be boys."

She wrinkled her nose. "I wouldn't know what to do with a houseful of boys!"

"I'll help you. So will Don Juan. Between the three of us, we can raise boys."

Bobbi looked down at Don Juan. "I'm not sure he's going to know how to raise boys *or* girls. I'm not sure if you noticed but..." She trailed off for a moment, and lowered her voice to a whisper. "He's a dog!"

"No!" Wilber shook his head. "He's *much* too intelligent to just be a dog. Maybe he's one of the fairies in disguise!"

She laughed, resuming their walk. They were close enough to the lake that she could see it through the trees. She wanted to stick her feet in it. "When are you going to take me rafting?"

"When are you going to agree to ride ATVs up into the mountains with me. I've been trying to get you to do that forever!"

"Forever? Sometimes I think you have problems with exaggeration, Wilber Weston."

He shrugged. "Oh, I really do. But especially when I'm talking about you, because I love you so much!"

She sighed. "Give me a few more days, would you?"

"So if I give you a few more days, you'll agree to marry me?"

She shook her head, not in answer to his question, but wondering what she should do about him. One thing she knew for certain. He was a good distraction from thinking about her father.

Bobbi opened the door of the spa, thinking they should have added it years earlier. She was seldom around to use it now, as it had only been open for a year. She went to the front desk and smiled at her daughter-in-law. "Please tell me there's been a cancellation and I can have a twelve-hour massage."

Maddie laughed. "I don't know about twelve hours, but I could make an hour and a half happen in about ten minutes."

"Are you kidding? I didn't think there was any way I'd be able to get in."

"I'm as surprised as you are. We had a cancellation a few hours ago. The guest had a family emergency and had to head back to West Virginia three days earlier than planned. She was not happy."

"Well, I'm not happy that she had a hard time, but I have to be pleased about my good fortune. I need that time on the table, thinking about nothing and letting my muscles be massaged into oblivion."

"Sounds good to me." Maddie waved a hand toward the water with orange slices floating in it. "Have some fruit water, or I can get you a root beer. I have a few stashed in the back for just such an occasion."

"A root beer would be absolutely wonderful. Do you mind?"

"Not at all. Have a seat, and I'll bring it out to you."

As soon as Bobbi was on the table, her mind wandered once again. Remembering just what had made her fall in love with the man who was now her husband was helping her remember why she needed to *stay* married. For a while, she'd thought she'd have to stay married for her six children, but it was more than that. She needed to stay married for her.

She'd been at the ranch about two weeks, and all the furor had died down over her father's escape from prison. On a Sunday afternoon, Wilber asked her if she'd go for a ride on the ATVs with him. He'd spent time teaching her to ride them, and she'd become proficient. She didn't enjoy leaving poor Don Juan behind, but his mother promised her that she'd take care of her pet.

So she agreed to go, looking forward to finally seeing the views from atop the mountain that overlooked the ranch. She met him outside after she'd changed out of her church clothes, and saw that he had a picnic basket with him. She was glad, because she was starving, and she knew he'd learned to always serve chocolate if they were going to eat together.

She climbed onto the ATV and started it. "Why do they have three wheels?" she asked.

He shrugged. "No idea. I hope someday someone invents one with four wheels. I think I'd feel a bit safer." He led the way up into the mountains, stopping at a picnic table about halfway up. "I thought you might be hungry."

"Have I ever not been hungry? Face it, I'm a bottomless pit!" She wasn't ashamed of it, because she was slender. She must have hollow legs, because there was no other explanation for where she put the sheer amount of food she ate.

They ate together, laughing over some of her stories from the diner. She'd started waiting tables, and she felt good about herself for the first time in years. "A man I'd never seen before came into the diner, and he wanted the day's special. The special was liver and onions. I don't know what your mother was thinking. I tried to tell him, but he wouldn't listen to me. So I took him out the special, and he wrinkled his nose, but he knew he was in the wrong, so he made himself eat every bite. Your mom and I giggled about it."

He laughed. "The pool is done, so they're breaking ground on the first of the cabins. I'm excited that it's finally happening. This was one of my ideas."

As they chatted, she realized that she was no longer nervous around him. He made her feel completely at ease, and she loved spending time with him. "Can we look for Bigfoot after lunch?" she asked, her eyes lit up.

"What's your obsession with Bigfoot?" he asked.

She shrugged. "I just think he's really cool, and if he does live in this area like I've heard, I want to be the one to find him. Is that so wrong?"

"I guess not. But think about this. If you find him, is telling people about him the right thing to do? What if you ruin his entire life, and even his ecosystem by telling scientists about him. They'll just want to study him, and then where will you be?"

She frowned. "Fine, then I'll just know where he is and

not tell anyone. When our kids are old enough, I'll be able to tell them without a shadow of a doubt that Bigfoot lives in our mountains."

He leaned forward and kissed her.

"What was that about?"

"It was the first time you've referred to our children as if having them is a foregone conclusion. I liked it."

She grinned. "I didn't mean to say it that way."

"I know you didn't. That makes it even more special, because you did it without thinking about it first. That means you really believe it. I guess it's time for me to start planning my proposal."

"You aren't supposed to tell me when you're planning a proposal! I'm supposed to be surprised by it!"

Wilber grinned. "But if I surprise you with it, how will you be able to practice your reactions?"

She laughed. "Do you want a big wedding?"

"I want whatever you want. If you want to run away and get married by a justice of the peace, then that's what I want. If you want to have a big wedding and invite everyone we've known since kindergarten, that's fine too. All I care about is you being happy. So do what will make you happy."

She looked at him with stars in her eyes for a moment. "What did I ever do to deserve you? I can't imagine that I ever did anything good enough to deserve the kind of love you give me."

"You were born. You came to Idaho. That's good enough for me."

"You really do know how to make a girl feel special."

He shrugged. "My mama was careful to raise young men with manners."

"She did a very good job." She leaned forward and pressed her lips to his, getting bolder with him every day. She knew she was going to marry him, and she saw nothing wrong with a bit of kissing before they were married.

"Mrs. Weston, your massage is over."

Bobbi yawned, startled. "Already? You just started!"

Andrea, the newest member of the spa team there on the ranch, laughed softly. "I promise I gave you the full hour and a half. I'd keep going, but I have another client due here in five minutes."

"I'd better hurry and dress and get out of your room then, huh?"

Andrea nodded. "That would be really nice."

As she walked back to the cabin, Bobbi felt a sense of peace come over her. She'd tell the kids about her father getting out of prison, and she'd let them decide if they wanted to meet him. They had every right to meet their grandfather, and they had never met their grandmother to hold her death against him. No, it was time to give them the choice, and she would abide by whatever they said.

It was a huge weight off her shoulders to not make the decision. She would be able to move on with her life and deciding whether she and Wilber were going to make it. Not that there was any doubt in her mind when she walked into the cabin and saw wildflowers everywhere. He loved her. What more could she ask for?

7

Bobbi spent the next morning helping out at the Kids' Korral. It was one of her favorite places on the ranch, and not only because three of her grandchildren were there all day. She arrived early in the morning. "I'm here to hold babies," she announced.

Debbie laughed. "You're welcome to hold babies all day if you want. Are you willing to feed and diaper them as well, or will you just sit quietly and hold them?"

Bobbi grinned. She liked Debbie a lot. They were close to the same age, and she enjoyed talking to her. "I will do whatever you need. It doesn't even have to be babies, though I would like a few minutes to hold my granddaughters."

"Go ahead and start out in the baby room then. Tori is being true to form and wiggling the morning away, while Willow sleeps. Tori could use some extra cuddles from Grandma."

"Just think, you'll be on grandma duty soon, too."

"I'm not sure I'm ready for that!" Debbie grinned as Bobbi disappeared into the baby's room.

Bobbi found Tori lying on a mat on the floor on her

tummy, wiggling like crazy and fussing at random intervals, then smiling broadly. She scooped the baby up and walked over to one of the gliding rockers, snuggling her close.

Tori looked up at her with the Weston ice blue eyes, a look of laughter filling them. "How's my baby? How's my little girl?"

Tori started giggling, which surprised no one. "You are the happiest baby in the whole world, aren't you?"

The baby teacher, Alexis, laughed softly. "Willow's a pretty happy baby too. They aren't old enough to get excited when their mother comes, but they do! She comes in to feed them around ten-thirty every morning, and I could swear those babies can tell time. They start wiggling and giggling about ten-twenty."

Bobbi let Tori sit up on her lap as she liked, and she thought back to when her twins were that small. Tori was just like Dani, always sitting up and wiggling and trying to do more than she possibly could for her age. Willow was more like her mama, happy to just be there. Kelsi seemed to dress them as if they were like her and Dani as well. Willow would wear pretty pastels and always had a bow in her hair. Tori wore darker, more "masculine" colors.

She rocked the baby back and forth, and her mind wandered off to many years before. She and Wilber had made it farther up into the mountain than she'd ever been, and she stood looking down at the ranch in awe. "I can't believe all that land belongs to your family."

He grinned. "We're about to buy that area over there, too. It's been in the Cooper family for generations, but their only son, Tim is in prison and probably never getting out. He's a wastrel."

She frowned, thinking of her dad. Was he a wastrel too? "Does your family constantly buy land?"

"Yeah. If it's on the border of the ranch, and it goes up for sale, we're the first in line to buy. There's so much more we want to do. The Coopers' land we're buying will eventually be made into a row of houses. We'll rent them out or use them for employees. Not sure yet, but we'll put it to good use."

"I'm stunned by the magnitude of the ranch. It seems like so much for just one family to be in charge of."

He smiled. "That's why we need lots of sons, and we need to raise them to love the ranch as much as we do. We need help running the place."

"What about daughters? Daughters can help too, you know!"

"I won't forget the daughters, but I sure hope the boys come first. If the girls are as beautiful as their mother, I'm going to be beating potential boyfriends off with a stick, and it would be nice if I had sons to help me!"

She grinned. "You sure do know the right things to say to reach my heart."

He pulled her against him, her back to his front, and just wrapped his arms around her waist. "I could stand here like this with you forever."

She leaned back against him, completely at ease. "If we stand here like this forever, how will we search for Bigfoot?"

He laughed. "You and your Bigfoot obsession. I hope our children don't inherit that from you."

"Why not? I think at least one of them should join me in my search for Sasquatch."

"If you say so."

She turned around in his arms and wrapped her arms around his neck. "It can't be just the two of us looking for him forever, after all."

"I don't have a choice in the matter, do I?"

She shook her head. "Not until one of the children joins my quest. Then you can stop."

He leaned down and kissed her softly. "If we're now

talking about our future children, don't you think it's time for us to start talking about a wedding date?"

"Not yet. I want to just enjoy being a couple for a little while longer. Marriage starts the years of work and raising children. Can't we just be in love for a while?"

He froze, staring into her eyes. "That's the first time you've told me you love me. Do you mean it?"

She grinned, nodding emphatically. "Of course, I do. I don't think there's a girl alive who could resist falling for you. Why, if Mother Theresa had met you as a young girl, she'd have fallen in love too!"

He laughed. "I'm not sure I could have convinced a devout nun to leave her course of life. I wouldn't have fallen for her, after all. You were the one the fairies sent to me. I know that because Jaclyn told me."

She brushed her lips against his. "Are we going to believe Jaclyn and her fairies? Or are we going to decide for ourselves?"

"Well, I believed her immediately, but you seem to be taking your own sweet time. We've known each other forever, and my ring is not yet on your finger."

"Ring? You haven't shown me a ring."

He reached into his pocket and pulled out a ring box. "I've been carrying it since a couple of days after I met you. Do you want to see it?"

She bit her lip. She did want to see it. Of course, she did. But…she also wanted to be surprised when it was time. "No, I'll wait."

"Are you going to let me know when I'm allowed to propose?" he asked. "I don't know how else I'll be able to tell that I'm supposed to."

"I'll make sure you know when I'm ready." Bobbi knew she didn't need a lot more time, but a bit longer would make her very happy. She was in love and enjoying it. Marriage would come...soon. But not today. She needed more time to just enjoy being in love.

Tori wiggled in Bobbi's arms, reminding her where she was. She jiggled the baby on her knee, overwhelmed at the idea that this baby would never have been born if not for her love for Wilber. The second generation was being born now, and she was going to love every second of it.

When Kelsi came in to feed the twins, Bobbi moved out of the second chair. "They're all yours."

"Thanks, Mom. What are you doing here?" Kelsi asked as she quickly began to nurse Tori.

"I came to see my grandbabies today. Willow slept all morning, but I played with Tori."

"Willow's a really good sleeper. Tori is a wiggler. Is there any doubt about why I called her Princess Wiggles?"

"None." Bobbi walked over to peer into Willow's crib, seeing her lying wide awake with her fist in her mouth. She unlatched the crib and picked the baby up, cooing to her softly. "I'm going to change your diaper, and then your mama's going to feed you the good stuff. Are you getting hungry?" The girl was dressed in a pink dress, complete with a bow in her hair. Tori was wearing blue overalls with a green shirt. "You never leave anyone in question of who's who."

"Well, they're not identical, but they do look quite a bit alike. It's just easier this way."

Alexis walked over as Bobbi finished changing Willow. "Do you want me to take her?"

"No, I'll hold her until Kelsi's ready for her. Then I'm going to run over to the school-aged children and steal Vivian. I think she needs a grandma day, don't you?"

"You just want to spoil her rotten. What are you planning?"

"Oh, I thought I'd grab a four-wheeler and take her up

into the mountains to search for Bigfoot. It's time to get the next generation interested, don't you think?"

Kelsi nodded emphatically. "I got the twins onesies that say, 'Bigfoot doesn't believe in you either.' Blue for Tori and pink for Willow. If they have matching outfits, they're never the same color."

"I didn't mean to scar you girls for life by dressing you alike. I thought that's what you did with twins."

"We'll get over it. Five or six years of intense therapy should do just fine."

Bobbi sighed. "I think you're about to learn that babies don't come with manuals. You just do what you think is right at the time, and pray that they don't hate you when the therapy bills start to come in." She handed Willow off to Kelsi and picked up Tori, who had fallen asleep while nursing. "I'm going to change her diaper, and put her to bed."

"No, Mom! If you change her she'll wake up and think that a five-minute nap was enough. Just put her down and she'll be fine."

"If you're sure..."

"I'm the mama this time around." Kelsi blew a kiss at her mother.

Bobbi did as she was told, slipping the baby into the crib and securing it. "I know you are, and I'll do things just how you want." She leaned down and kissed Kelsi's cheek. "Now I'm going to steal Vivian, so we can go Bigfoot hunting. She'll love it."

"Did you have Bob make lunches?"

Bobbi nodded. "They're waiting at the café. We'll pick them up after we get the four-wheeler."

"You're not letting her ride her own?"

"I may be blonde, but I'm *not* stupid!" Bobbi hurried from the room before Kelsi had a chance to retort. She loved her youngest child, but she was quick with comebacks.

When she got to the room for the school-aged children, she found Vivian curled up on a sleeping bag, reading a Nancy Drew book. "Haven't you read all of those yet?"

"I'm close. I'm starting on Trixie Belden next."

"I thought maybe you'd like to go on an adventure today."

Vivian nodded slowly, obviously a bit apprehensive. "What kind of adventure?"

"Well, I thought we'd borrow a four-wheeler, get a picnic from the diner, and go up into the mountains to search for Bigfoot."

"You know Bigfoot's not real, don't you?"

Bobbi shook her head. "He's as real as you and me. I saw him in the mountains one day, right after I married Grandpa. We're going to find him."

Vivian sighed, shaking her head. "Grown-ups are so easily duped. Let's go."

Bobbi quickly spoke to the teacher and told her what the plans were. She knew she was on the list to take Vivian out of the Kids' Korral, so that wouldn't be a problem. After she was finished, she looked back at Vivian. "Okay, we're all clear!"

They two of them left the center hand-in-hand. Vivian had her book tucked under her arm so as not to lose one precious minute of reading time. They got the four-wheeler and two helmets, a blue helmet with a star for Vivian, and a lavender helmet for Bobbi.

They rode over to the café in silence, and went in to pick up the lunches Bobbi had ordered that morning. "We're going on an adventure," she announced to Joni, who was behind the counter.

Joni pushed the boxed lunches at Bobbi. "I hope you have a wonderful time, Mrs. Weston."

"I'm sure we will. I have the best companion in the world, you know."

Vivian was beaming as they walked out to the four-wheeler. "Are we taking a picnic blanket?"

Bobbi frowned. "We can run by the cabin to get one if you want."

Vivian nodded, her face very serious. "I need to have some place to lie on the ground and read while you hunt for Bigfoot."

Bobbi sighed. It was just as well. One of the other grandchildren was sure to share her fascination with Bigfoot. She wasn't about to give up. "We'll get a quilt from the cabin, and then we'll go on our adventure."

"Where's Grandpa?"

"I'm sure he's off pestering your dad and telling him he has to do something differently. That's what he's *always* doing at this time of day."

"How come? He seems like a nice Grandpa."

"Oh, he is! His parents did the same thing with him, and their parents before them. As frustrating as it is, that's just how things are done at the ranch."

"My dad won't. When it's his turn to pass it on to his kids, he's going to be nice about it and not be so mean. I know it." Vivian accepted the quilt Bobbi gave her and hugged it to her chest, climbing back onto the four-wheeler. "I'm ready."

Bobbi frowned at the girl before getting on. She'd never really questioned the practice before, other than being frustrated about it with Wilber when they were going through it. Maybe it was time someone did.

As they drove along the winding path that took them to the area she wanted to picnic in and where she'd search for Bigfoot, her mind couldn't stop thinking about what the little girl had said. Sometimes children were so much smarter about things than adults were.

She had spent many days all those years ago following this same trail up the mountain with Wilber, and they'd both loved it. They would climb, and he would immediately pick her a bouquet of wildflowers.

One afternoon, he tucked a flower behind her ear. "There. That flower brings out your natural beauty."

Bobbi had laughed, shaking her head. "No, that flower is the beauty."

He cupped her face in his hands. "I wish I had the ability to let you see yourself through my eyes. I look at you, and I see someone that I'll never stop loving. I see someone who I will spend my entire life with, never caring to look at another woman. I see none of your past, which seems to be all you see when you look in the mirror. I see the real you, and I wish I could show it to you." He kissed her softly, his arms wrapping tightly around her. "I wish I could paint, so you could see what I see."

Bobbi felt tears drifting down her face. "My grandparents couldn't even look at me after my mother's death. They said they looked at me and saw only the man who had killed their daughter. I think maybe I've been looking at myself through the same tainted glasses they were using."

"Stop. Please."

She took a deep breath. "I'll try. I can't make any promises, but I'll try."

"That's all I ask." He kissed her once more, quickly. "Well, that and for you to marry me, of course. You need to marry me."

Bobbi wrinkled her nose. "You know I'm waiting for a real proposal. I'm not going to let you ask me to marry you that way and agree."

"Does that mean you're ready?" he asked, an eyebrow raised.

"Maybe. I'll let you know."

He sighed. "You're always going to let me know. Always."

She shrugged. "Well, I never said I was perfect."

"No. I did."

Bobbi pulled the four-wheeler off the path and stopped at a big meadow. The wildflowers grew abundantly, and she grinned at Vivian. "Let's pick all the flowers before we put the picnic quilt down. We don't want to squish them."

"And I can give them to my mama!"

"I think that's a great idea. She'll be so happy!"

"I know she will!"

Together, they hurriedly picked flowers, making two huge bouquets. "This one is for my Grandma."

Bobbi sniffled, taking the flowers. "Thank you, sweetheart."

"You're welcome. Thank you for coming to take me out of the Kids' Korral today. It's fun to play there, but it's more fun to have a grandma day with you."

Bobbi hugged the girl. "Okay, we'll put the bouquets on the four-wheeler, and then we'll spread the blanket out. Are you ready?" They each took one end of the blanket. "One. Two. Three!"

They fluffed the blanket up into the air and then gently set it down. Bobbi put the boxed lunches into the middle of the blanket. "I should have thought to bring the picnic basket. Wouldn't that have looked nicer?"

"It'll taste just as good!"

"That's true. And we know it'll be yummy because Bob made it. Bob can be a pain, but he sure can cook!"

"That's the truth," Vivian said, looking at the boxes to see which had her name. Bob remembered the tastes of everyone, and always customized their lunches to suit them.

She pushed Bobbi's box toward her. "I think he included root beer, Grandma!"

"He certainly should have! He knows we Westons can't eat a meal without a swallow of root beer."

Vivian nodded solemnly. "And I'm a Weston now."

"Yes, you are. So root beer it is!" Bobbi popped the tab back on her drink, then traded with Vivian. Once they were both holding a root beer, she clinked her can against Vivian's. "A toast. To happiness."

"To happiness," Vivian echoed, taking a swig of the root beer. "Yummy!"

They got down to the serious business of eating, both of them hungry after the long trip up to their picnic spot. "When I was a little girl, I wanted to be a ballerina," Bobbi said.

"Why weren't you? You're as pretty as a ballerina."

"I'm not exactly what you'd call graceful. My mother put me in lessons for a little while, but I kept tripping over my own big feet. We decided the art wasn't for me."

Vivian giggled. "Grandpa loves you anyway. He gives you the same kind of look my dad gives my mom. The look that always makes them kiss."

"Yes, your grandpa loves me a great deal. Do you know we've been married almost thirty-five years? That's almost forever!"

"That's longer than my dad is old!"

"Isn't that a coincidence?" Bobbi said with a sparkle in her eye. "I'm glad you're happy here at the ranch."

"Everyone is happy at the ranch," Vivian said matter-of-factly. "The ranch is a happy place. People would have to *try* to be sad here."

"It really is a special place, isn't it? I think I'm going to stay here forever."

"But you live in an RV with Grandpa. You're just visiting for a while. I know because I heard Aunt Kelsi telling Kaya."

Bobbi frowned. "That's been the plan. You see when I agreed to marry Grandpa, we decided that we were going to travel the world as soon as our children were old enough to run the ranch. So we have been driving from state to state, trying to see as much as we could. But now that we have grandkids, I want to spend more time on the ranch to be with them."

"Does Grandpa want to?"

Bobbi shrugged. "He loves you grandkids as much as I do, but he doesn't want to stay here all the time."

"Well, then you should do it some of the time. It's as simple as that."

"Maybe you're right."

8

That evening, Bobbi got home just after Wilber arrived. "Where were you all day?" he asked. "I was planning on taking you out for dinner, but I didn't know where you'd disappeared to."

Bobbi wasn't sure if he sounded more annoyed or concerned. "I'm sorry. I should have let you know what my plans were. I went to the Kids' Korral today to hold the twins, and then I kidnapped Vivian, and we had a picnic up on the trail."

"I see. I wish you'd told me what you were going to do."

"I'm really sorry. I would never deliberately frighten you."

"Well, do you want to go for trivia night? I hear that the pastor and Bridget are teaming up with Kaya and Glen, and between them they know some serious trivia. I'd love to team up with Bob and Miranda."

"Bob and Miranda? They're only going to know cooking questions!"

He shrugged. "So what? At least we'll have fun."

She nodded. "Sure. Let me just change out of my picnic

clothes." She could see some grass stains on the knees of her jeans.

As she was leaving the room, he caught her arm, spinning her toward him. Pushing her up against the wall, he lowered his mouth to hers. "You're beautiful just the way you are. Never change."

Bobbi felt her face softening, and she wrapped her arms around his neck. "You make me feel like I'm a teenager sometimes, Wilber Weston."

"You always make me feel like a teen." He leaned down and nipped her neck before backing away. "Hurry, so we can go."

She slipped into the bedroom to change quickly, her face heated from their embrace. He really did make her feel like a teenager very often. But then she'd look around and see her children and grandchildren, and she'd remember she was a middle-aged woman.

She changed into a pair of nice slacks and a silk blouse. It was a little dressy for the restaurant, but it would be fine. She loved to mingle with the guests on trivia night, finding out what activities they were still enjoying and which should be overhauled.

Wilber was leaning against the wall waiting for her when she came out. "You didn't have to stand there waiting."

"How else could I escort my beautiful bride to dinner?" He noticed she wasn't wearing a necklace, and then his eyes landed on the one he'd given her a couple days before, still on the coffee table where he'd set it. Somehow she'd never opened it. He walked over and picked it up, bringing it to her. "Maybe this would go with your blouse?"

She took it, her heart beating faster. She couldn't believe that in the confusion with her father's letter that she'd forgotten to open his gift. She carefully opened the box, and gasped. There lay a necklace that she'd told him she wanted,

FOREVER FAMILY

but she never dreamed he would actually get her. It matched her blouse perfectly. She'd always loved pink diamonds, but she never let herself indulge. "Thank you! It's perfect." She held it up to her neck and turned around so he could fasten it for her.

"I always feel so clumsy trying to fasten these things. My hands are too big!"

"I appreciate you trying. If you can't do it, I'm sure someone will do it at the restaurant."

"I got it." He fussed with it for a little longer, before finally fastening it.

"Thank you!" She turned to him and kissed him quickly. "How did you even know?"

"I saw you looking at it while we were in town a few weeks ago. It suits you. I was going to wait to give it to you at our anniversary party, but I thought it would be nicer if you could wear it there."

She hadn't yet decided if there was going to be an anniversary party, but he was obviously doing everything he could to make it happen. She could not fault his efforts. "It's absolutely gorgeous."

He slipped his arm around her waist and they walked across the grounds toward the ranch house. It was the same place where she'd stayed when she first arrived in Idaho, and where they'd raised their children. The decision to add a restaurant had been made when all four boys had moved out and across the street. Now there were a few guest rooms, a couple of rooms for the staff, a library, a living area, and the restaurant.

"Do you ever wish we'd kept this as our family home on the ranch?"

He shook his head. "Not at all. I couldn't have let just one of the kids live here, and there was no reason to even try. It makes a lot more sense that we're using it for other things."

She smiled. "I really thought you'd be more sentimental about it. You and your brothers were raised here, and we raised our children here."

"We have some pretty incredible kids."

"And beautiful grandchildren."

He frowned at the mention of the grandchildren. He knew it was still her desire to be there and watch them grow that was keeping them apart. He'd have to figure out a compromise quickly. He wasn't about to let her go. "Have you decided what you want to do about your father?"

"I'm going to ask the kids on Sunday, and leave the decision entirely up to them. They have the right to know their only living grandparent if they choose to."

"So will you have them vote?"

She shrugged. "I guess so. I hadn't thought that far ahead. I just thought I'd tell them the situation and let them discuss it amongst themselves." She waited as he opened the door to the restaurant for her before moving over to sit with Bob and Miranda. "Wilber is certain the four of us will be unstoppable."

Miranda laughed. "Maybe if we added my mom, or my brother, or someone with some sort of knowledge of trivia..."

Bobbi grinned. "At least we'll have fun, right?"

Miranda was right, and their team was absolutely horrible. They finished second to last, only barely beating out a group of twenty-somethings from Riston. After the first round was over, Bobbi stood. "I'm going to go mingle and talk to the guests. See what they're liking this year, and what they think should be changed."

"That's not our job anymore," Wilber told her, his voice low.

"I know, but it's fun!" Bobbi walked to the next table and smiled at the group of women gathered there. "I'm Bobbi Weston. Do you mind if I sit down for a moment?"

Twenty minutes later, she was still sitting with them, listening to them gush about their favorite activities on the ranch. "Is there anything you'd like to see us add?"

Two of the women exchanged a look, and one of them finally nodded. "We were saying it would be really fun if you had different craft nights. Like Monday could be for quilting and everyone could take home a quilt block. Tuesday could be scrapbooking. And you need to sell special River's End Ranch paper in the general store. That would be so fun! Then a night for crocheting and another for knitting or baking. Charge a little bit for each activity, and I know everyone would love it."

Bobbi nodded, smiling. "That's a wonderful suggestion. Don't be surprised to see us doing it if you come back next year." She stood and walked back over to her husband, knowing another round was about to start. She quickly passed on what the woman had said before the next question was asked.

At the end of the night, Bobbi was full of root beer and nachos, ready to head back to the cabin. As they walked, Wilber wrapped his arm around her waist. "Did you have fun?"

She nodded. "I had a fabulous time. We were awful, but it was fun. I can't believe there was a whole section of Bible questions on the night Pastor Kevin was there. He said God was rewarding him for his faithful service, but I think he rigged it somehow."

Wilber laughed, shaking his head. "I don't think so. It was just fun."

"I guess." Bobbi was highly competitive, and she hated to lose. At least she'd had fun getting to know Miranda and Bob better. "Are you judging amateur night tomorrow night?"

He shook his head. "No. I traded weeks with Wade. He

said something about needing to be off next week. I don't remember why."

"You really should pay better attention when the kids talk to you."

"I pay good enough attention. Wade never knew I was daydreaming about how beautiful my wife was while I was talking to him."

Bobbi shook her head. "Are you trying to get yourself out of trouble?"

"I don't know. Is it working?"

She laughed. "I've missed just hanging out with you. We've always seemed to have to be somewhere and doing something lately. Just spending time together has been at the bottom of our list."

He stopped walking and turned to her. "I'm so sorry I've made you feel that way. Since the day I met you, you were the most important thing in my life. That hasn't changed."

"For me either." She stepped closer to him and hugged him, losing herself in his embrace. It sounded like his feelings hadn't changed at all...just how he demonstrated them. That should be good enough for her.

That night, after Wilber was asleep, she lay in bed thinking back to his proposal. She'd been on the ranch for just under a month when she'd realized she was ready. Bobbi sat with Wilber eating lunch in the diner on Saturday, and as they held hands, she leaned forward. "I think I'm ready for that question you've been wanting to ask me."

Wilber's eyes lit up. "Are you sure?"

She nodded. She was still enjoying their relationship, but things were getting more heated between them, and because she didn't believe they should go any further than kissing until they married, she knew it was time that they move to the next step. "I'm sure."

"May I come and get you after the diner closes, then?"

She nodded, her heart in her throat. He was going to ask her that night. He'd had a few weeks to plan how he'd ask, so she was excited to see what he did. "Should I change first?" she asked.

He shook his head. "Absolutely not. I love you just the way you are."

She grinned. "I'll remind you that you said that when I'm old and gray."

"You won't have to. I'll never forget."

He was there with his pickup truck when the diner closed that afternoon. Leaning down to kiss Kelsey's cheek, she said, "I'm going to spend the evening with Wilber. Don't hold dinner for me."

Kelsey smiled. "Have a nice time."

She hurried out to the truck and slid into the passenger side, wishing he could kiss her, but knowing his mother was watching. He drove out of the parking lot and off the ranch, surprising her. "I figured you'd ask me here at the ranch."

"You gave me lots of time to plan the perfect proposal. Now you're going to get it." He drove down the highway, and up into the mountains.

On the other side of the mountain from the little valley where the ranch was, she saw a huge lake. "Oh, that lake is beautiful!"

He kept driving, surprising her. "Where exactly are you taking me?" she finally asked.

"Not telling."

She pouted, leaning back in her seat, but still he drove on. He finally stopped on the side of the highway, putting his truck into park. "Will you go for a walk with me, Bobbi?"

She nodded, unsure of what was so special about this place, but she slipped out of her side of the truck. He plucked a picnic basket from the bed of the truck, and took her hand in his.

He walked down a steep bank, and she saw a creek cutting through the land, which was covered with wildflowers. There were more than she'd ever seen, there for the picking. "Oh, this place is beautiful!"

He nodded. "I scoped it out last week, hoping you were getting close to being ready." He led her down to a quiet area beside the creek and spread the picnic blanket he'd tucked under one arm out.

He carefully set out the food he'd brought, which looked like a small feast to her. There was fried chicken, potato salad, and root beer. And at the bottom of the basket, she saw a couple of brownies. It was the same thing he'd packed for their first picnic. "Everything looks delicious."

"It will be. I promise." He took her hand and brought it to his lips, kissing it softly. "I made sure everything was perfect for tonight."

"I can't imagine it being better than this," she told him. As they ate, he talked about what he wanted from the future. Plans for the ranch and plans for a family together.

When they'd finished eating all but the brownies, he took her hand in his. "The day you walked onto the ranch, my entire world changed. Never have I loved something or someone more than I loved the ranch I was raised on. Until you. From the first moment I saw you, I knew you were meant for me. I knew you were the woman I was supposed to grow old with, to love forever. There's nothing in this world that would make me as happy as you agreeing to be my wife." He moved until he was kneeling in front of her. "Bobbi, would you do me the great honor of being the mother of my children and the woman who sleeps beside me every night?"

Bobbi swiped at the tears streaming down her face. "I would be delighted."

He wrapped his arms around her and held her close. "Oh no!"

"What?" What could possibly be wrong with him at that moment?

"I did it wrong. I forgot to have the ring in my hand."

She laughed softly. "No, Wilber. You did it just right. The ring doesn't matter. It's the man who's proposing that I want to spend my life with. Not an engagement ring."

"Well, I still have to give it to you." He pulled away from her and dug into his pocket, pulling out the ring he'd purchased shortly after she'd arrived. He opened the box and held it out for her to see. "May I put it on your finger?"

Bobbi stared at the ring in surprise. "I expected a diamond."

He smiled. "It is a diamond. It's a pink diamond. It seemed to suit you better than a clear one."

"I love it. It really does suit me."

He slipped it onto her finger, and then brought her hand to his lips. "This ring is a symbol of my love for you. I hope you'll wear it for the rest of your life."

"I can't imagine ever taking it off. I love you so much, Wilber!"

He kissed her, his hands going to her back and stroking her. "When?"

"When what?"

"When are you going to marry me? Have you spent your whole life dreaming about a big wedding? Or can we run away to marry tomorrow. There's no waiting period in Idaho..."

She laughed. "I suppose tomorrow works for me. Will your mother be hugely disappointed if we don't have a big wedding?" She couldn't imagine making him wait for the wedding. He'd already had to wait before she'd let him propose.

"No, she won't mind at all." He stood up, and pulled her to her feet, holding her close. "I can't believe I'm going to wake up and see your face on the pillow beside mine for the rest of my life."

"You don't snore, do you?" she asked, her brow wrinkled.

He shrugged. "No idea. Maybe? Would you hate it if I did?"

"If it's part of you, how could I hate it?"

"I like that answer." He kissed her softly. "And after our kids are grown and running the ranch themselves, we need to take off in an RV and see the country. There are so many states I've never seen. So many things I've never done. Promise me we'll do those things together."

"I promise!"

Wilber let out a loud snore, bringing Bobbi back from her memories. She'd meant what she said all that time ago...but lately, *she'd* been different. It hadn't been him that had changed. It had been her. Her dreams had changed, but his had stayed steadfast, which was a good word to describe her Wilber.

She propped her head up on her fist and watched her husband sleep. He made her smile. He made her so happy. She couldn't begin to imagine life without him. As soon as he woke up, she was going to tell him that she'd been wrong. She would travel with him just as much as he wanted. And they would have their vow renewal right there on the ranch as they'd been planning.

She grinned as she thought of the way Dani had gotten angry with her and stood up to her about the lavender Chinese lanterns. Of course, they hadn't been for Dani. She knew her daughter better than that. Bobbi, however, loved the color lavender, and she couldn't wait to have the lanterns decorating the area around the gazebo where she planned to dance until dawn with the man she loved. The man she'd always love.

Wilber stirred, to find Bobbi watching him sleep. He turned toward her with a smile. "What?"

"I was just thinking about how much I love you, and about the promises we made each other when I agreed to marry you. I said that I'd travel the country in an RV with you, and that's what I'll do. Seeing the grandbabies on holidays and during visits here will just have to be enough for me."

He shook his head. "No, it won't. I have a better idea."

She raised an eyebrow. "If it means me seeing the grandbabies more, I'm all for it."

"Why don't we spend every other month here, and every other month on the road. You can see your grandbabies grow up, and we can both see the country as we've always wanted to do."

"But that's not what you want!"

"Of course it's what I want! I love those grandbabies too, but more importantly, I love you. This is a way we can both be happy."

She squealed, wrapping her arms around him and kissing his face all over. "I love that idea! Are you sure it's okay with you?"

"I'm positive. Now can we get back to planning our vow renewal? Maybe it's time to tell the kids what all the improvements have been for? Partially to test them, of course, but mostly so we could have our vow renewal right here on the ranch. You haven't canceled anything, have you?"

Bobbi shook her head. "Of course not. I wouldn't have without discussing it with you first."

"Good. Then on Sunday, we'll tell them about your father wanting to get to know them and about our vow renewal. Bad news with good news? Though I'm not quite sure your father wanting to meet them is bad news."

"I'm really not sure either. I think it's up to them to make of it what they want. I've decided that even if the kids don't want to see him, I do. I want to talk to him. It's been so long, and he's never been anything but kind to me. I have to stop hating him for what happened all those years ago. He's done his time. It's time for me to learn to forgive."

Wilber stroked her cheek. "Are you sure? No one is going to fault you if you can't forgive him. It's a pretty big thing to forgive someone for."

"I'm sure. I've been thinking about it constantly since I got his letter. That and us. We decided long ago that we were meant to be together. Or the fairies did, anyway."

He laughed. "I don't believe in the fairies any more than you do, but if they make Jaclyn happy, who am I to complain? She's been so kind to us and to our children. I'm sure she'll someday be matching our grandchildren."

"Do you think so? She's not immortal, you know."

"I'm not so sure! She and Mom were the same age, but Mom always looked older. I think the fairies have given her the gift of everlasting life."

"I think you've lost your mind!"

"I lost my mind over you a very long time ago. I hope I never find it again." He pulled her closer, wrapping both arms around her and holding her against him. He was keeping her. Nothing was going to come between them again.

9

Bobbi woke up early the following morning and reached over for Wilber's arm, but he wasn't there. She sat up in bed, frowning. He hadn't told her he needed to be somewhere early.

She got up and wandered through the small cabin, calling his name. Finally, on the coffee table, she found a note.

My love,

Meet me in front of the cabin as soon as you're dressed and showered. No peeking until you're ready. Dress casually.

All my love,

Wilber

She frowned and walked to the window. He knew she wouldn't be able to resist one peek. He wouldn't even be surprised. With as long as they'd been married, it was like he could read her mind.

She lifted the curtain out of the way, surprised to find a piece of cardboard taped over the window. "I said no peeking!" was written on the cardboard.

Bobbi laughed, shaking her head as she walked back toward the bathroom. Obviously, he'd done everything he could to keep her from looking. She hurried into the bathroom and showered and dressed. She wished she could force herself to take her time, but she was much too excited to see what he was up to.

She put on a pair of jeans and a T-shirt before running a brush through her hair. She'd never been one of those women who took hours fussing as they stared at themselves in the bathroom mirror.

Twenty minutes after opening her eyes, she was ready. She hoped Wilber had thought to get them something to eat.

She stepped out the front door to see her husband leaning back against a four-wheeler. There were two there in front of the cabin, ready for them to use. "Did you think about breakfast?" she asked.

"We're going to head to the diner to pick up our lunch, so we'll go ahead and have breakfast while we're there. If it was kolache day, I'd have a bag in my hand waiting for you to devour."

She grinned at him. "Well, I'm happy to have breakfast with the man I love. Are we walking over or four-wheeling?"

"Oh, four-wheeling. I know the exact kind of chariot my queen desires."

She laughed, sitting down on the one with her helmet. "Did you walk over to get one and then walk over to get the other?"

"Oh, no! I reminded Wyatt about the arthritis in my hip, and casually mentioned that I walked the floor with him and changed his diapers. He wrinkled his nose, but he knows he's about to start that nonsense, so he was willing to drive one over and walk back himself."

"Oh, good job playing the parent-with-arthritis card! I'm impressed at the way you think!"

He shrugged. "I learned from the best!"

She laughed, taking the lead as they drove across the

ranch, stopping in front of the diner. "Looks like we missed the breakfast rush. Good. Maybe it won't be too crowded."

He stopped his four-wheeler and removed his helmet, hanging it off the handlebars. Taking Bobbi's hand in his, he led her to the restaurant and opened the door for her. As soon as they were seated, Kelsi brought menus over. "Breakfast special is eggs in a hole with your choice of bacon, sausage, or corned beef hash."

"Sounds good. Eggs over medium. Hash." Bobbi looked at her daughter, whose eyes were looking a bit bloodshot. "You okay?"

Kelsi nodded. "Willow was fussy all night, so I was up with her."

"You need an assistant manager." Bobbi knew all new parents went through periods of no sleep, but she wished her daughter had the ability to stay home from work when it happened.

"I have Joni. She's going to close this afternoon, so I can go home at two instead of four."

"Good! I'm so glad you have someone you trust."

Kelsi looked at Wilber. "What are you having, Dad?"

"Huckleberry pancakes with a double side of bacon and a cup of coffee."

"I want orange juice," Bobbi added.

"All right. I'll get Bob to start on these and get your drinks out to you." Kelsi walked away, her usual zip missing from her steps.

"If she wasn't nursing, I could take the babies overnight. But neither of them will take a bottle." Bobbi frowned at her husband. "How am I supposed to help her if she's trained them not to take a bottle?"

"Obviously she's done that, because she'd rather feed them herself. Just let her handle things. I'm sure Shane helps as much as he can."

"He's a good husband to her." Bobbi shrugged. "I just feel like I should still be taking care of my babies." She looked down at their joined hands on the table for a minute. "I think that's a lot of the reason I married you. I needed a family I could be part of forever, and I knew you'd give that to me. You and your parents, and any kids we had. And then we got Jess as a bonus."

"I know. I knew it at the time. You loved me, but you loved me partially because I could provide you with that forever family."

After they'd eaten, they headed for the door, and Jess was waiting on one of the four-wheelers, something held in her arms. "I brought you a present, Aunt Bobbi. Uncle Wilber said you needed it more than you realized."

Bobbi frowned and looked at her niece, just then realizing what she was holding. "A puppy!"

Jess nodded. "It's a little boy. He was abandoned, and someone brought him to us."

Bobbi took the small animal and cuddled him against her, loving the feel of his fur against her chin. She had tears in her eyes. "This is exactly what I needed. How did you know?"

Wilber grinned, shrugging. "When you mentioned Don Juan the other day, you had such a wistful look on your face. I knew you needed a new puppy to love."

"I do! I really do!" She held the puppy out so she could look at him, noting that he was almost entirely white. "I'm going to call him Galahad. It makes him the perfect successor to Don Juan."

Jess hurried forward and kissed her aunt's cheek. "I'm going to take him to spend the day with me at the clinic. I know you two have other plans, but I wanted you to see that he was yours."

Bobbi walked over to Wilber and wrapped her arms around his neck, kissing him. She'd never been demonstrative in public, but she didn't care about her stupid rules at the moment, and it didn't matter how many guests saw them. Her husband deserved something for the special gift.

Wilber held her close for a moment. "You ready?"

"Sure. Do you have lunches?"

He nodded, patting the seat of his four-wheeler, and she knew that he'd put their boxed lunches in the compartment under the seat. "Let's be off then."

They rode side by side up the trail, but she let him lead in the places where the path was too narrow. When they reached the spot where she'd picnicked with Vivian, she expected him to stop, but he just kept going.

Finally, he stopped in the spot where she'd first convinced him to help her hunt for Bigfoot. "Are you ready?"

She frowned at him. "Ready for what? It's only been an hour since breakfast. I'm not ready for lunch."

He shooed her off her seat and pulled a bag out from under it. It was the bag she'd put together when she'd first initiated Kelsi into Bigfoot hunting. It held several artists' renditions of Bigfoot and a magnifying glass. There were even examples of Bigfoot's hair for them to use for comparison.

"Does this mean what I think it means?"

"Well, I know you wanted to Bigfoot hunt yesterday, and your usual partner is now tied to a couple of babies..."

She threw her arms around him and hugged him again. "What have I ever done in life to deserve you? I'm so sorry that I got persnickety this week. You are the only man who would ever not only put up with me, but continue to love me through my moods. Thank you for being you!"

"Does that mean you like my plan for the morning?"

She laughed. "It sure does!"

They wandered all over the area of the mountain where she was sure Bigfoot would be found. After several hours of constantly looking, she wiped some sweat off her brow and took a swig of the water he'd given her. "I'm done for today."

"Let's eat our lunch then. I have stuff planned for this afternoon."

She eyed him curiously. "What stuff?"

He shrugged. "Nothing major."

Somehow, she didn't believe him, but she didn't argue. After their picnic, which consisted of fried chicken, potato salad, and brownies, along with cans of root beer, she shook her head at him. "Sometimes the details you remember just amaze me. We had this on our first picnic."

"We did. I wondered if you'd remember."

"Of course, I do!" Bobbi remembered more than he gave her credit for, but the truth was, she didn't give him much credit either. She was going to start focusing on the good in her husband and not the negative aspects of him.

"Okay, it's down the mountain with us. We'll return the four-wheelers, and then we have to take a ride in the truck."

Bobbi didn't argue. He'd obviously planned out this day, and she wasn't going to argue with him. She got onto her vehicle and buckled her helmet on. "Let's go."

As they drove down the mountain, she carefully avoided the bumps in the trail that she knew like the back of her hand. During the years when she'd been having babies every couple of years, she'd missed her time in the mountains. As soon as the twins were old enough to be left with her in-laws for a period of time, she was off hunting for Bigfoot again.

After returning the four-wheelers to the ranch's rental area, they got into his truck. "Where are we going now?"

"As if I'm going to tell you that. I think you know better!"

Bobbi grinned, looking over at her husband and not seeing the hair that was gray at the temples or the little laugh lines around his eyes. No, she saw the same handsome man she'd met at the ranch thirty-five years before, and she was so happy to have him in her life.

As they drove west, over the mountains, she looked over the lake that was in the next valley over. She'd always been fascinated by the beauty of the area, but she'd never been willing to leave the ranch for her recreation. That would be like living in paradise, but needing another paradise to visit to be happy.

When Wilber slowed the truck, she realized where he was taking her. To the spot that was filled with wildflowers, where he'd asked her to be his wife. He walked around the truck and helped her down, keeping her hand in his as he walked her to the exact spot.

"Wilber, we're already married."

"I know. But I always felt like I did that proposal just a little bit wrong." He led her to the spot beside the creek where they'd had their picnic, and got down on one knee.

"Oh, Wilber, don't hurt your hip!"

He shook his head. "Forget about my hip. Forget about everything but what I'm saying to you. My life began the day you walked onto the ranch and into my mother's café. Every day of my life since then has been centered around you. You've helped me fulfill dreams I didn't even know I had until we met. And now, we've been married for so long, I have to ask you...will you marry me again?" He reached down and pulled a ring from the pocket of his jeans. "Will you spend the rest of your life exploring the world, hunting for Bigfoot, and visiting grandbabies with me?"

Bobbi swiped away at the tears drifting down her face. She nodded as she held her hand out for the ring he held, waiting for him to slip it on her hand. It was much like her original engagement ring, in that they were both pink diamonds. However, this one perfectly matched the necklace he'd given her the night before. Both had the same heart-shaped cut to them.

He slowly got to his feet and gathered her against him. "This time you'll have the wedding you deserve. If you need more time to put it together, that's just fine. We're going to have fun with it."

She shook her head. "No, I don't need any more time. I have everything I need all ready." She'd been slowly adding things to shipments for a year, without letting Dani know why. She had everything she needed. Invitations would go out, and they would have a vow renewal by the end of the month.

Bobbi waited until everyone was finished with their family dinner on Sunday before she said anything. The café was filled with laughter and love, which was how she liked it. She'd raised children who were respectful to their elders and who loved their siblings beyond belief.

Bobbi got to her feet, and reached her hand out for Wilber's who took it, lending her his strength. "I have a couple of things I need to talk to you all about." The café was immediately quiet, as she knew it would be. "First of all, I want to tell you why we've been so crazy about certain things being done here on the ranch. Like having a full-time pastor for weddings, and setting up the event barn. We wanted everything perfect for our vow renewal, which will be taking place at the end of the month."

Dani got to her feet first. "Is that what those lavender Chinese lanterns were about? I thought you were losing your mind!"

Bobbi laughed. "That's exactly what they were about, but

it's almost over. I mailed out invitations yesterday, and by the end of the month, your cousins will be swarming the ranch."

Wade shook his head. "Do we have to be nice to them?"

Vivian giggled. "Dad!"

"Just checking!" Wade said with a sigh.

"I'd like Jess, Dani, and Kelsi to be my bridesmaids, and Vivian, I'd like you to do me the honor of being my flower girl."

Dani wrinkled her nose. "Do we have to wear matching dresses?"

Bobbi rolled her eyes. "Would it kill you for one afternoon?"

"Maybe..."

"No, you don't have to wear matching dresses. I found a pattern that was simple, but elegant. I ordered one for you in a dark blue, ice blue for Jess, and one for Kelsi in a pink. You don't even have to wear the same color."

Kelsi grinned. "You're the best!"

Bobbi shook her head at them. "You two are silly." She looked over at Wilber, and he gave her a nod, which told her it was time for the other announcement. "The other part of what I have to say is harder. You all know that my father has been in prison for the past forty-five years, and why. Well, he's going to be getting out three days before our vow renewal, and he wants to meet all of you. I'm going to meet with him, but I'm going to leave it to all of you whether or not you want him to be a part of your life. I'll understand any decision you make."

10

There was silence for a full minute as everyone processed what Bobbi had just said. Finally, Wilber broke the peace. "We've decided that you can vote or each decide individually if you want to meet him. Your mother has made her decision, but this isn't something she can decide for all of you."

Kelsi stood up. "He's my grandfather, and he has a right to meet my babies. I want to meet him."

Shane shook his head at her. "I don't like it."

Kelsi glared at her husband. "You're the sheriff. Wear your gun."

Wes frowned, but finally nodded. "Yeah, I think we should all meet him. There's strength in numbers. We're tall, strong, and fast. He's what? A hundred?"

Bobbi glared at her son. "He's about the same age as Jaclyn."

Travis leaned forward. "How old *is* Jaclyn, anyway?"

Dani swatted Travis's arm. "None of your business. I'll meet him, Mom."

Wyatt nodded. "I'm in. We'll all meet him together. I

agree with Wes. Together, I don't think we have anything to worry about."

Amber looked at Bobbi. "Why not just invite him to the vow renewal? It'll be a renewal between the two of you, but also a renewal of your relationship with your dad."

Bobbi looked at Wilber. "Why didn't we think of that?"

He shrugged. "No idea, but it's a good idea. Let's do it."

She took a deep breath and nodded. "Is there anyone who isn't willing to meet him?"

When no one spoke up, she nodded. "That's what we're doing, then. I'll invite him to stay at the ranch and give him a room in the main house."

"Are you sure that's safe?" Shane asked, always thinking about protecting others.

Bobbi stood for a moment and dug deep, thinking back about everything she knew about her father. Finally, she nodded. "I'm sure. I'm very sure."

"Okay. You know him best."

There was a buzz of excitement that hadn't been there before Bobbi had made her announcements, and everyone came over to talk to her one by one, each of them sharing their excitement.

Bobbi finally cut it short. "We have to go. Galahad has a puppy-sized bladder, and he needs to be let outside or there will be puddles...and no untrained dogs are allowed in the cabins. I know because I made that rule myself!"

Everyone laughed, and she waved as she headed out with Wilber beside her. "I think that went really well," he said once they were out of earshot of all the others. "Are you pleased?"

She nodded. "I really am. I don't think I realized until now just what compassionate children we've raised. My dad's going to be so proud of them."

"Just like we are." He held her hand in his as they walked

back toward the cabin they were staying in. "If that dog tore something up again..."

"Galahad loves you, and he's just trying to get used to his new home..."

THE NEXT TWO WEEKS FLEW BY, AND BOBBI WAS IN HER element. She got everything ready for the wedding, and went to dress fittings with Jess and the twins.

"I guess these dresses aren't terrible," Dani said, tugging at the fabric to try to make it drape differently.

"I like mine," Kelsi said, glancing in the mirror. "This pink looks so good with our coloring and our Weston eyes."

Jess simply nodded, happy with hers. She'd always complained a great deal less than her cousins anyway.

Bobbi ignored them as she looked in the mirror while wearing her dress. She'd gone with a wedding dress, but not a floor-length dress. She wanted something she could dance in. Instead, she was wearing a tea-length off-white dress with her cowboy boots. What else would be perfect for a ranch wedding?

As the days got closer, she got more and more nervous about her father's arrival. She'd arranged it so she and Wilber would have dinner with him in Riston, before he ever set foot on the ranch. This was her sacred place, and if she sensed even a bit of danger from the man, he wouldn't be allowed on the ranch, father or not.

Finally, it was Friday night, the day before the vow renewal, and she was headed to Riston, her hand clutched tightly in her husband's. "I'm nervous."

"I know you are...but remember, he's the man who pushed you on the swing and called you his princess. He's the man who escaped from prison so he could find you."

She took a deep breath and nodded. "Do you think he's already there?"

"I have no idea." Wilber parked the truck in front of the small restaurant where they'd chosen to meet. "But I do know we can handle this together. We've had six kids and raised seven. We have grandchildren coming out our ears. We've run our ranch for years. We've got this."

"You're right. If I could raise those children of ours, I can do anything." She slid out of the truck to the ground, and waited as he locked the vehicle. They joined hands and together, they headed into the restaurant.

The hostess—an old friend of Kelsi's—recognized them immediately. "Mr. and Mrs. Weston, it's good to see you!"

Bobbi smiled. "We're meeting an older gentleman tonight."

"Oh, he's been here for two hours. He was afraid of being late, he said." The hostess led them to a table back in one corner of the place, with a lone man with gray hair sitting at it.

The man was looking down at a book resting on the table, and didn't notice them there at first. All at once, he looked up, and his eyes filled with tears. "Bobbi."

"Hi, Dad." She felt her own tears start to flow, feeling like a fool. She'd been the one keeping them apart. She could have visited him any time.

He slowly got to his feet and she walked to him, burying her face in his shoulder. "I didn't think you'd come," he said, even as his arms came around her, holding her tightly against him.

"I wasn't sure if I would either," she said honestly. "Let's sit." He sat back down in the chair he'd occupied before. "This is my husband, Wilber."

Wilber offered his hand to shake. "It's nice to meet you, sir."

The old man laughed. "No one has called me sir in a very long time, I'm afraid. My name is Reggie."

Wilber took his seat across from Bobbi, his hand automatically taking hers across the table. "The grandchildren and great-grandchildren are all ready to meet you tomorrow."

"Six children, right?" Reggie asked, his eyes lighting up at the thought.

Bobbi nodded. "I gave birth to six, but we also raised my niece, Jess, so we say seven."

"And how many grandchildren do you have?"

"Three with more on the way," Bobbi said softly. "My youngest had twins in February. She's a twin as well, but hers are fraternal, but she and her sister are identical."

"I was a twin," her father said, surprising her.

"I never knew that!" Bobbi said. "I don't think I ever met your family."

"My sister died when we were young, and my parents never really got over it. So I didn't have a lot to do with them. They blamed me for her death."

"Why?" Bobbi said a silent prayer that they weren't about to find out he'd killed his sister as well.

"Because it was her and not me. There was no other reason. I assure you, I've only killed one person in my life." He shook his head. "I never meant to kill her."

She nodded. "I know that. I think I even knew it at the time." She sighed. "When Mom's parents refused to look at me, because I reminded them of their daughter's killer, I just kind of broke. All of the foster homes wanted me to get out as fast as I could, except the last one. They were trying to fix me."

"You were never broken." He sighed. "I haven't touched alcohol since the day she died. Even before they arrested me, I had none. I never will again."

"I'm glad," she said softly. "It took me a lot of soul-searching to decide to come here. But I finally decided that I'd grown up without parents, through no fault of my own. I wasn't going to deprive myself of my father when I had a choice."

"So tell me all about you. What have you been doing for the last forty-five years?"

Bobbi laughed softly. "I've been raising babies, the most important job I've ever had. Let me tell you about my children..."

LATE THE FOLLOWING MORNING, BOBBI WAS STANDING IN the back of the small church in the middle of the Old West town she and Wilber had envisioned so many years before. She was surrounded by her daughters and her niece. "I don't know why I'm nervous. It's not like I haven't done all this before—with the same man, even."

"You're nervous because your dad is here this time," Kelsi said. "How did dinner go last night?"

Bobbi smiled. "It was very nice. I talked to him about you kids. He feels terrible for what happened all those years ago, so we talked about it for a minute and moved on. He's very excited to meet his grandchildren."

"Do you think he'll move to the ranch?"

Bobbi's eyes were sad as she shook her head. "He may for a month or two, but he told me last night that he has pancreatic cancer. He's not going to live longer than that."

Kelsi stepped closer to her mother and hugged her close. "You just found him again."

Bobbi nodded. "I don't want to say goodbye, but at least I won't spend the rest of my life wondering what exactly happened. Or what would have happened if I'd just let him in."

Dani said nothing, but she squeezed her mother's hand.

Jess frowned and whispered, "I'm so sorry, Aunt Bobbi."

"We're not going to let today be sad, though," Bobbi told them. "I'm renewing vows with the man I've loved for two-thirds of my life. And I'm celebrating a reunion with my father. We're going to see people we love, and we're going to eat, drink, dance, and be merry."

"Mom, I don't think dance is supposed to be in there..." Kelsi told her.

"It is in my world."

Pastor Kevin stuck his head back into the tiny area where they were crowded. "We're starting."

Behind Pastor Kevin was her father, offering his arm. She took it and watched as her three girls walked down the aisle. "They're going down in order of age," she whispered to her father. "Jess is first, then Dani, and then Kelsi, my baby."

"Where are Kelsi's babies?" her father asked.

"They're with Shane, their father, sitting at the back of the church, because he expects them to have him up and down."

Then it was time for her to walk to the front of the church on her father's arm. It was something she'd never imagined doing, but she did it with pride. Every eye was on them, and when she reached the front of the church, she kissed her father's cheek before turning to Wilber. He was the only man she'd ever loved, who had gotten her through the hard times of her life. She would never be able to live without him.

Bobbi danced with everyone at the reception—her father for the first time in almost half a century—her sons, her sons-in-law, her nephews, and many of the ranch employees. But most importantly, she danced with Wilber.

She made her way around the tables, where everyone feasted. She broke tradition and decided to serve two meals, so they could dance until dawn if they chose to. She stopped by one of the tables to see several of the Weston cousins who had spent every summer on the ranch, harassing her children and being harassed in return.

"Hello, you three!"

Kenneth smiled at her. "Hi, Aunt Bobbi. Congratulations on marrying Uncle Wilber a second time. Just don't have more sons, okay?"

Bobbi laughed. "I think I'm past my child-bearing years. Thank God. Now I get to be a grandmother and send them home after they're good and spoiled."

Kenneth's sister, Marybeth, grinned. "Those babies of Kelsi's are just adorable!"

"Aren't they sweet?"

Cooper shrugged. "I guess if you're into mooning over babies, they're okay."

Bobbi just laughed. "Are your parents here? I haven't seen them?"

"They couldn't make it. They were going to come, but Mom had emergency gall bladder surgery, so she sent us on without her," Marybeth said. "I feel like I should be there helping out, but Dad said he had it."

"Give her my best." Bobbi made a mental note to send a get-well card as she moved on to the next table.

Kelsi was sitting with Shane and the twins, talking softly to the babies. "Mom!"

"Kelsi!" Bobbi laughed and shook her head. "Your cousin Athena looks like she's sitting alone over there." Athena's real name hadn't been quite good enough for her, so she'd changed it. Her hair was down almost to her bottom, and she wore beads as a headband. She was odd, which was why Bobbi would prefer it if Kelsi was the one to deal with her.

"Yeah, I tried to talk to her, but she was mumbling something about herbs that would make my milk come in faster, and I got out of there. I'm nursing twins. My milk is just fine, thank you very much!"

Bobbi grinned. "Maybe I can talk Dani into going over and talking to her."

"Good luck with that! She's too busy making cow's eyes at Travis."

Bobbi shook her head and gave up. If Athena couldn't make a move to talk to the others, she wasn't going to force one of her children to go and talk to her. She glanced at her niece once more and saw that Jaclyn's nephew was there talking to her. How the nerd and the hippie would get along, she didn't know!

Instead, she walked across the crowded dance floor, and stopped in front of her husband. "I think this dance might have to be mine."

"Oh?"

She nodded. "I haven't felt your arms around me in at least an hour. What happens if I shrivel up and die for lack of your love?"

"You know as well as I do that it doesn't matter if I'm with you or not. My love is there."

She sighed happily. "I do know that." She looked over her shoulder for a minute. "Do you realize that many of the people that are here today, wouldn't be without our love? Marrying you did exactly what I needed. It gave me my forever family."

ABOUT THE AUTHOR

kirstenandmorganna.com

ALSO BY KIRSTEN OSBOURNE

To sign up for Kirsten Osbourne's mailing list and receive notice of new titles as they are available text 'BOB' to 42828

CPSIA information can be obtained
at www.ICGtesting.com
Printed in the USA
BVHW080853171119
564073BV00019B/1193/P

9 781978 049611